Look for
Dog Lov[...]
by Melissa Cleary

A TAIL OF TWO MURDERS
Jackie finds a beautiful dog with a bullet in its leg . . . and, not much later, the dead body of her boss at the Rodgers U. film department . . .

DOG COLLAR CRIME
Dog trainer and basset hound devotee Mel Sweeten is killed with a choke collar—and Jackie and Jake have to dig up the facts to find out whodunit . . .

HOUNDED TO DEATH
Mayoral hopeful Morton Slake has the morals of an alley cat—but when his girlfriend is found dead, Jackie and Jake prove that every dog has his day . . .

SKULL AND DOG BONES
An ex-screenwriter says goodbye to Hollywood after someone spikes his bottled water . . . and Jackie's on her way to L.A. to solve the case!

FIRST PEDIGREE MURDER
After Mannheim Goodwillie's voice hit the Rodgers U. radio airwaves, he hit the floor—and now Jackie and Jake are trying to pick up the signals of a killer . . . "Absorbing . . . quick and well-written."—*Armchair Detective*

DEAD AND BURIED
Walter Hopfelt's job was keeping the Rodgers U. campus safe from crime. But now the security chief's career is over—along with his life . . . "Mind candy for dog lovers with a fondness for mysteries."—*Sun-Sentinel (FL)*

THE MALTESE PUPPY
Jackie has her hands full finding a home for Maury, Jake's gigantic and badly behaved puppy. It's even harder when she's trying to solve a murder at the same time . . .

MURDER MOST BEASTLY
The bizarre death of a Palmer zookeeper proves to Jackie that not all the so-called animals are behind bars . . .

OLD DOGS

MELISSA CLEARY

BERKLEY PRIME CRIME, NEW YORK

OLD DOGS

A Berkley Prime Crime Book / published by arrangement with
the author

PRINTING HISTORY
Berkley Prime Crime edition / July 1997

All rights reserved.
Copyright © 1997 by The Berkley Publishing Group.
This book may not be reproduced in whole or in part,
by mimeograph or any other means, without permission.
For information address: The Berkley Publishing Group,
a division of Penguin Putnam Inc.
375 Hudson Street, New York, NY 10014

The Putnam Putnam Inc. World Wide Web site address is
http://www.penguinputnam.com

ISBN: 0-425-15858-6

Berkley Prime Crime Books are published
by The Berkley Publishing Group, a division of Penguin Putnam Inc.
375 Hudson Street, New York, NY 10014.
The name BERKLEY PRIME CRIME and the BERKLEY PRIME CRIME
design are trademarks belonging to Penguin Putnam Inc.

PRINTED IN THE UNITED STATES OF AMERICA

10 9 8 7 6 5 4 3 2

OLD
DOGS

CHAPTER 1

"They're going to throw her right out on the street, Jackie! How can we let them do that?"

"Oh, come on, Mom," Jackie Walsh argued as she stepped out on her back porch and handed her mother a glass of iced lemonade, "Forest View Convalescent Home isn't going to put an eighty-two-year-old woman out on the street. No one does that sort of thing any more. Even if she runs out of money, I'm sure they'll make some sort of arrangement for her."

"A state hospital is what sort of arrangement they'll make," said Frances Costello. "She'll spend the rest of her life in some awful, dirty, overcrowded hospital ward with a lot of crazy people. It breaks my heart to think of it."

Jackie's mother, a sprightly woman of seventy-something, had recently begun volunteering two afternoons a week at Forest View, a convalescent hospital on the outskirts of Palmer, Ohio. "Those old people need cheering up," she had told her daughter, and Jackie certainly couldn't argue the fact that if someone needed cheering up, Frances Cooley Costello would do the job or make them wish she had.

"Well, I'm sure it'll work out." Jackie hadn't exactly been giving her full attention to her mother's story about

the problems of Winnie Swann, a Forest View patient she'd
become fond of since she began her volunteer job. With
Frances, she'd learned in thirty-eight years of being her
daughter, it was always something, usually trouble, and often as not she didn't particularly want to be involved.

It was a beautiful spring day in the tiny backyard of
Jackie's downtown Palmer, Ohio townhouse—part of a
renovated industrial building that had become an urban du-
plex of tall, narrow loft apartments when the old neighborhood had gotten a face lift a few years back.

Jackie liked her unusual apartment with its tall windows,
high ceilings with exposed pipes painted in vibrant colors,
and its proximity both to the campus where she taught and
most of the leading cultural attractions of the city. Years
of stagnating in the suburbs had made her yearn for a place
just like this. She'd used her savings to buy it for herself
and her young son, Peter, taken her collection of vintage
movie posters out of storage and relocated them on the red
brick walls of her living room and loft bedroom, and proceeded to make herself thoroughly at home.

Having delivered refreshments, she busied herself throw-
ing a rubber ball to her German shepherd, Jake, who never
seemed to tire of running after it. He returned to drop it at
her feet, wagging his long, bushy tail eagerly until she
picked up the ball and threw it again.

Jackie was grateful that her mother had discovered something to alleviate her loneliness since her best friend, Bara
Day, had married her ardent suitor, given up on midwestern
winters, and gone to live in Florida. Soon after that the
circle of women that used to meet once a week for poker
had slowly begun to drift apart, and Frances had become
restless. The Forest View volunteer job had been one good
thing for her, and joining a local book club run by Jean
Scott, the Palmer Gazette book reviewer, had been another.
Nothing could keep Frances down for long.

"I'm not sure it will work out at all," Frances grumbled.

"In my experience when large institutions take care of things, they're done with the least attention to human needs and the most attention to the bottom line. I don't think for a moment that things are run any differently at Forest View. Anyway, at least say you'll bring Jake to Pet Day tomorrow."

"Pet Day? Is this something we've discussed, Mother?" Jackie was immediately suspicious of her mother's casual mention of some upcoming special event. She racked her brain for a memory of a previous conversation, but try as she might, this was the first she could remember hearing about it.

"Of course we have," Frances assured her with a look of total innocence. "Good heavens, Jacqueline, you don't think I'd just drop something like this on you with one day's notice, do you?"

Jackie did think exactly that, but she decided to let it pass. "What exactly is Pet Day anyway?" she asked her mother.

"Once a month the volunteers bring in animals for the patients to play with. Sometimes they get the animal shelter to lend them kittens and puppies, or they have staff and volunteers bring pets from home." Frances began to warm to the subject. "You know, Jackie, you'd be amazed what relating to an animal does for these people. Even the ones who're pretty far gone with Alzheimer's can really perk up when you put a kitten or a puppy in their lap. It's just that little spark of life that seems to make all the difference."

"Have you thought about taking Aloysiüs?" Frances had given her python, Victor, to Bara as a wedding present so Bara's python Scalia wouldn't be lonely in Florida, and replaced him with a Mexican boa. Jackie suspected at least part of the reason must be that the boa, much smaller and lighter than the portly Victor, was easier to lug around.

"Very funny. You know Al's not exactly crazy about

strangers, Jackie. Besides, I think he's getting ready to molt.''

Jackie suppressed a smile. ''And he's not exactly the warm and cuddly type, either, is he?'' she asked, knowing what her mother's reaction was bound to be.

''Snakes are extremely cuddly!'' Frances objected. ''It's just that most people don't understand them. And I have to put you in the category of 'most people' where that's concerned.'' Frances sniffed indignantly, but Jackie could tell she wasn't really angry. ''Just say you'll bring Jake tomorrow. He's such a sweet dog, and I know Winnie would love him.''

Jake picked up his large ears at the sound of his name, then returned his interest to the ball when it became evident that the familiar word was not a prelude to either a snack or an outing. Jackie watched him trot back across the yard to deposit the ball on the grass in front of her. ''Well, tomorrow's Wednesday, so I don't have class, and my office hours end at two. I could be at Forest View by two-thirty. How would that be?''

Jackie taught film classes at nearby Rodgers University— a course called Film and Society this semester—which she was enjoying a great deal. It was a bonus when you got to do something you loved for a living, she often reminded herself, and Jackie loved the movies. She tossed the ball again in the direction of the fence, and Jake bounded after it.

''Two-thirty would be terrific,'' said Frances. ''That having been taken care of, my darling daughter, how's your love life?''

''Quiet.''

''Boring, you mean. Haven't heard from Ronald lately?''

''No, and I don't think I'm going to. That whole thing hadn't been going too well for a long time, you know— even before Ronald had to fly off to Prague.'' Jackie's former boyfriend, the veteran television actor Ronald Dunn, had seemed all too happy to use the excuse of a European location shoot for his latest film, a big-budget Hollywood epic, to leave Palmer, Ohio and Jackie's company for greener pastures. The spark had long since gone out of the romance, if indeed it had ever really been there in the first place, and after all those years in Hollywood, at the center of the entertainment industry, he'd found life in a quiet midwestern city more than a bit boring. It had taken him no time at all to pack his bag, make his excuses, and catch the next available plane.

The surprising thing, Jackie thought, was that she really hadn't been all that sorry to see him go. It had been glamorous, she supposed, dating a well-known actor, but there wasn't a lot to Ronald once you got past the immediate surface, which hadn't taken very long.

"Well, I never thought he was the one for you anyway," said Frances, and Jackie may only have imagined the hint of smugness in her voice. "What I do think is that you're too young not to be out there finding a replacement for him. Whatever happened to that detective of yours?"

Frances was referring to Michael McGowan, the tall, blue-eyed police detective Jackie had been involved with before she had hooked up with Ronald, and with whom she had solved quite a few local murder cases over the last couple of years. "He wasn't *my* detective, Mother," Jackie said. "And he's in Hollywood writing for a television series. I still hear from him now and then, but it's over."

She wondered if that was really the way she wanted it, but it wasn't entirely her decision, after all. She had been the one to end the relationship, but at the time she'd walked into his apartment and found him in bed with another woman—a beautiful blonde dog handler whom Jackie had always felt a bit intimidated by—there hadn't seemed to be any other choice.

She had always felt more than a little guilty about the fact that she had actually spent the previous night with Ron-

ald Dunn, a fact she had neglected to mention to Michael
when she ended the relationship, and hadn't had the moral
courage to bring up in the months since then. If that hadn't
been the case she probably wouldn't have been nearly so
righteously indignant at Michael's behavior. They didn't
really have an agreement, in so many words, not to see
other people, but neither of them had been honest with the
other, and that was a very bad sign for any future she may
once have had in mind for them. "There's nothing going
on there, really," she said, and neglected to catch the sigh
that escaped when she said it.

"Well, there ought to be something going on somewhere, Jacqueline," her mother said, shaking a finger at
her in what Jackie thought of as one of her more irritating
habits. "You're a young woman. Attractive, too. You look
just like my mother when she was your age, and she was
a great beauty, you know."

"Yes, Mother, I know." Jackie hurried to agree with
Frances before she could launch into a long reminiscence
about her mother—the great beauty Julia Shannon Cooley—
her grandmother, and ancestors even further removed. "But
I'm fine, really. I'm alone, sort of, but I'm not lonely, and
it's kind of nice not having to worry about anyone but me
and Peter for a change. And Jake, of course."

She tossed the ball across the yard, but Jake had grown
tired of the game and watched with utter indifference as
the ball bounced off the far fence and came to rest on the
grass. He walked to the edge of the yard and began pacing
restlessly up and down the length of the fence. After six or
seven trips up and down the little yard he whined once,
walked over to a shady spot and lay down with his head
between his paws.

"Well, what do you suppose is the matter with him?"
Frances wondered.

"I don't know," said Jackie, "but he's been acting like
that a lot lately. Maybe I should take him to see Jason."

Jason Huckle, a local veterinarian, served as Jake's private physician. He'd once had a mild crush on Jackie, but they'd long since gotten over any discomfort about that, and had settled down to a comfortable, if not exactly close, relationship. If there was something wrong with Jake, Jason would surely be able to figure out what it was.

"By the way, are you doing anything special this evening?" Jackie asked her mother.

"I was thinking about renting some martial arts movies and making popcorn," said Frances. "There's a new Jackie Chan feature down at the Video Barn." She looked at her daughter over the tops of her gold-rimmed glasses. "Did you have something better in mind?"

Jackie didn't want to ask her mother if she was serious, but knowing her, that was exactly what she had planned for an evening's entertainment. "It's just that there's a reception at the University tonight for Dwight Hockersmith."

"That city councilman who's threatening to run for mayor?"

"I guess the threat has become a promise," Jackie sighed. "Olin Oliver seems to be involving himself in the campaign, and he wants to kick off with a getting-to-know-you party in the Political Science Department, and he's asked me to be there. I think he's afraid if the colleagues who owe him favors don't show, he and Hockersmith will be there all alone." Olin taught in the Poli Sci Department, and had once taken a stab at local politics, but with little success. Jackie didn't exactly consider him a friend, but he was a pitiful sort of man, and people seemed to go out of their way to make him happy just so they wouldn't feel so guilty around him.

"Well, anyone would be better for Palmer than Jane Bellamy," said Frances, shaking her head. Palmer's present mayor, a former instructor at Rodgers, was widely considered to be ineffectual at best, and possibly incompetent.

"Not necessarily anyone," Jackie cautioned. "As bad as

she is, there are plenty worse choices. Still, it won't hurt to check out Dwight Hockersmith. It'll make Olin happy, and it won't cost us anything.''

''Free food and drinks?'' Frances wanted to know.

''Of course.''

''Well, I'm not foolish enough to pass that up. I've found, though, over the course of a long life, that you usually have to pay for free food with outrageous amounts of boredom. Oh, well,'' she sighed, ''you're only young once. Count me in.''

''Great,'' said Jackie, relieved at not having to face the boredom of a political cocktail bash alone. ''I'll pick you up at seven.''

CHAPTER 2

Jackie was always just a little relieved to see her mother go, and always just a little guilty at her own relief. She stood on the porch, waving goodbye as her mother's car pulled away from the curb. Frances took a lot out of a person. It was difficult just trying to keep up with her level of energy, never mind staying one step ahead of her mental processes.

Fortunately the visits never lasted too long; Frances always had someplace to go and something to do. She had half a dozen important errands to run in the few hours before seven o'clock, and Jackie had no doubt she'd be raring to go at seven, and ready to party the night away when Jackie was dying to come home. Frances Costello was never bored, and certainly never boring. At least Jackie would get a few hours rest before she faced an evening with her mother at Dwight Hockersmith's kickoff reception.

"Mom, do you think Jake gets tired of just being an ordinary dog?" Jackie's thirteen-year-old son Peter had come home from school shortly after his grandmother left. Now he sat at the dining table with Jake at his feet, and scratched the big shepherd behind the ears and under his wide leather collar as Jackie thawed out some leftover lasagne for their dinner.

"Well, I don't know, Peter," Jackie began. She had to be careful to call him Peter now, and not Petey. He'd made it abundantly clear how much he hated his childhood nickname now that he was no longer a child. She still slipped up every now and again, but she was getting better. "I'm sure he had a lot more to think about when he was a working police dog, but people need a change of pace sometimes, and I'm sure that's just as true of dogs. Maybe he's enjoying his retirement." She couldn't help remembering, though, Jake's strange actions in the back yard earlier this afternoon.

Jake had wandered into Jackie and Peter's lives by accident a couple of years ago after a close call with the men who had murdered his former master, a retired police officer, and his life and theirs had never been the same since. "I have to admit he's been acting strange lately," she said, looking at the big shepherd lying at her son's feet. "I was thinking of taking him to see Jason."

"You think he's sick?" Peter examined Jake anxiously, as though for any sign of illness. "His nose is still wet."

"Always a good sign. In dogs, at least. No, I don't think he's sick, exactly, but maybe you're onto something. Maybe he's just bored. By the way, it's your turn to set the table," she added.

Peter sighed, predictably, but got up and walked into the kitchen.

"Wash your hands first," she reminded him, and was rewarded with another sigh, this one barely audible, as he turned on the faucet.

"Use soap," she told him.

"Mom!"

"Just kidding."

Peter washed up, took plates and glasses from a kitchen cupboard and flatware and paper napkins from the top drawer, and, stacking them precariously in his arms, walked over to the dining table and set them down, saving the entire construction from disaster with a quick move of his arm, as it started to fall. "Bet you thought those glasses were a goner," he teased. He flipped a glass up into the air and caught it, right side up, on the way down to the table top. "No problem when you're as great as I am."

Jackie watched her auburn-haired son with undisguised affection. Peter was maturing more than a bit this year, beginning to change from a cute little boy into a handsome young man. A growth spurt and karate classes had eliminated the baby fat he'd been plagued with the past few years. The kid whose idea of exercise was flipping through channels with a remote control was now working out six days a week. Best of all, his attitude had improved immeasurably. He was still a teenager, with all the attendant exasperation that tended to produce in a parent, but Jackie was beginning to think she might actually survive until he outgrew it. That had not been a foregone conclusion even six months ago.

"Jake may have enjoyed being ordinary at first," Peter went on, back on the subject of his dog, "but sometimes I get the feeling he'd like something more to do."

Jackie got the feeling it was Peter who wanted something to do, but that was all right, too. One of the good things about having a dog adopt you, as Jake had adopted Jackie and Peter a couple of years previously, was the way he seemed to provide endless opportunities for activities that had never previously been a part of their lives. "What did you have in mind for Jake?" she asked Peter.

"I thought maybe he could train for obedience trials, or something like that," said Peter, so quickly that Jackie was sure he'd just been waiting for the right question to spring this reply. "He can already do a lot of stuff dogs do in those, but this would be a little different—hurdles, and stuff like that. And competing against other dogs."

Jackie nodded thoughtfully. "He might enjoy something along those lines, I suppose." She looked out the kitchen window at the small backyard. "I don't think we've got much room here to set up a practice course, though."

"That's okay, Mom, 'cause there's a new kennel in town that has a course already set up."

"Where did you hear about that?" Jackie wanted to know.

"Career days, remember?" Jackie had recently taken her turn at speaking to Peter's eighth-grade class at the Downtown Arts School about her job teaching at Rodgers University, just as she did every year since she and Peter had come back to Palmer after a long and dreary stint in the suburbs with Peter's father, Cooper Walsh.

"This guy Tom Cusack came to school today—he's a dog trainer, and he bought that old kennel where that guy was murdered."

An involuntary chill went up Jackie's spine. She remembered the circumstances of that murder all too clearly. Well, the former Sweeten's Kennels had had a hard-luck past— maybe a new owner and a new identity would mark the end of it.

"I guess we should check it out . . ." she began.

"Tomorrow after school?" Peter jumped in.

"No, I've got to do a favor for your grandmother tomorrow. Pet Day at the convalescent hospital. Want to come along?"

"No thanks," Peter replied. "Maybe I'll just take a bus to the kennel after school and talk to Mr. Cusack for a while."

"Okay, but not until after you've done your homework, okay?"

"Okay, Mom."

"Promise?"

Peter crossed his heart solemnly, but couldn't seem to resist rolling his eyes afterwards. "Hope to die," he sighed.

A much-improved teenager, but a teenager nonetheless.

"Homework never killed anyone yet," Jackie promised her son, ruffling his hair in a gesture he grudgingly tolerated from her, "but sometimes it seems like it might. Anyway, you get me some details about this training thing and what it's going to cost me, and we'll talk about it some more tomorrow when I get home."

"But you will come and meet him soon?" There was no denying the eagerness in his request.

Jackie couldn't help wondering what stake Peter had in whether or not she met this Tom Cusack person. She eyed him thoughtfully, but decided against making a point of it. "As soon as I can," she promised him, and crossed her heart.

"Cool," said Peter, which seemed to settle it.

"So what seems to be the problem with the old boy?" Jason Huckle's voice was tinged with concern on the other end of the telephone connection. "Nothing serious, I hope."

"Probably not serious enough to bother you at home," said Jackie.

"Hey, you always know you can call me any time," said Jason. "Now, what's up?"

"Jake's acting strangely. Peter's noticed it, too."

"Define strangely."

"He's been listless, I guess, and kind of . . . I don't know . . . unsettled."

"Anything change in his life recently? New food, new input, new boyfriend, perhaps?"

Jackie was glad Jason couldn't see the expression on her face. "Absolutely nothing new," she told him. "In fact, Peter thinks that might be the problem. You know, maybe he's just bored."

"That's possible," said Jason. "I'd make it a point to watch for repetitive behavior, like barking or pacing. . . ."

"Pacing! He did that just today!"

"Okay. Stuff like that, and anything that just seems out of character or neurotic. Bring him in on Monday and tell me what you've noticed. I'll rule out any physical problems just as a caution, but my guess is Peter's right—the old boy is probably suffering from ennui. Happens to the best of us."

"What do you prescribe, in that case?" Jackie asked. She'd been feeling a little apathetic herself lately, what with Ronald out of the picture and the necessity of taking a look at her life. Maybe what worked for Jake would work for her, too.

"The very best cure for boredom is excitement," Jason said, chuckling. "And I know how much you like having excitement in your life. Maybe you and Jake just need another mystery to solve."

"Forget it, Doctor," said Jackie. "I've had enough of that to last me a lifetime. Jake and I will just have to find some other cure."

CHAPTER 3

Jackie had never been especially thrilled by—or even especially interested in—Palmer, Ohio politics, and the election of Jane Bellamy, former instructor in Rodgers University's Political Science Department, as mayor of Palmer hadn't done much to pique her interest. Palmer was largely run by the people in town with the biggest heaps of money—which didn't exactly set it apart from any other city, state, or country—and things hadn't gotten noticeably better during Mayor Bellamy's administration. If they had gotten any worse, Jackie hadn't noticed it.

Dwight Hockersmith was a Palmer boy—born, bred, and educated. A classmate of Olin Oliver's, he'd received his bachelor's in Political Science from good old Rodgers University, and had gone on to law school at Northwestern, returning to Palmer to practice corporate law and begin working his way up the political ladder.

Soon after being elected to the City Council, he'd begun to make quite a show of opposing Mayor Bellamy on the majority of issues, taking every opportunity to get his face on local television, looking properly dynamic and sincere, which had led to a certain amount of speculation on whether or not he might oppose Jane in this year's elections. To no one's surprise, he had decided to do just that.

As Jackie and her mother walked into the lovely old
nineteenth-century library in the R.U. Political Science Department that had been prepared for tonight's festivities,
Jackie could see Hockersmith, whom she recognized from
the amount of local television coverage he'd managed to
get himself lately, flanked by Olin Oliver on one side and,
on the other, a perfectly coifed blonde who looked far too
well turned out and respectable to be anyone but Mrs.
Dwight Hockersmith. Sighing, Jackie walked toward them,
preparing to pay, in the usual manner, for the champagne
and finger food Frances would consume this evening.

"Jackie! I'm so glad you could come!" Olin Oliver, or
"Oh, oh," as his students and a number of his colleagues
called him behind his back, seemed genuinely pleased to
see her. "Allow me to introduce you to the man I hope
will be the next mayor of Palmer, Ohio—Dwight Hockersmith. Dwight, this is Jackie Walsh, the rising star of Rodgers University's Communications Arts Department, and
sometime detective."

Jackie resisted rolling her eyes in exasperation at Olin,
and shook hands dutifully with the candidate, a tall, slender
man who looked to be in his late thirties, with curly light
brown hair and pale blue eyes, and tried to put as much
genuine feeling into it as she could muster. "I'm very
pleased to meet you, Mr. Hockersmith."

"Detective?" echoed Dwight Hockersmith. "Now that's
interesting. Do you work for the Palmer Police?"

"Olin's exaggerating," Jackie assured him. She fer-
vently wished she could kick Olin in the shin. "May I
introduce my mother, Frances Costello?"

"I'm very pleased to meet you both," said Dwight
Hockersmith, "and you must call me Dwight. When people
call me Mr. Hockersmith, I always think they mean my
father. Enjoy yourselves." He passed them in turn to the
rather formidably pretty Mrs. Hockersmith—Angela—a
perfect copy of every media-trained politician's wife in de-

signer clothes and a flawless blonde coiffure, who radiated
warmth all over them for exactly three seconds before turning to the next person in the line. That timer switch must
come in handy for gatherings of this sort, Jackie decided.
Maybe she should ask her where she got it.

Frances went to forage, and, mindful that she had to
drive home later, Jackie declined champagne and accepted
sparkling apple cider from a passing server. There was actually a pretty good turnout, she noticed, glancing around
the room at the assembled Palmer intelligentsia, such as
they were. Several of Jackie's fellow instructors were in
evidence at a glance, including Mark Freeman, who taught
animation in Jackie's department, and Keith Monaghan,
who taught radio arts and ran the campus radio station.
Both were pleasant and intelligent people, and either would
have afforded a few minutes of interesting conversation, but
before she had a chance to move from the spot, Dwight
Hockersmith was at her side, two *faux* crystal glasses of
sparkling cider at the ready.

"You looked like you might be ready for another of
these," he said, smiling.

"Well, I wouldn't want to get silly," said Jackie. "This
stuff's pretty dangerous." She emptied her half-full glass
and accepted the one he'd brought her.

"Oh, I can quit any time I want to," he joked, raising
his glass in a toast. "To Palmer."

"To Palmer," Jackie echoed. "Good luck in your campaign. Jane Bellamy's going to give you a run for your
money, I imagine."

"I wouldn't want it any other way," said Dwight Hockersmith. "Your mom, huh?" He indicated Frances, who
was engaging Olin Oliver in a lively discussion of some
sort, a plate of food balanced on either hand.

"She came for the free food," said Jackie.

"She seems to be quite a character."

"Oh, she hasn't even got started yet. But if you'd like

to see it happen, just open a conversation on the subject of Irish history. Take the side of the British Empire, if you really want some fireworks.''

''I think I'll pass,'' said Hockersmith, holding up a hand to ward off an imaginary Frances. ''My father's a handful, too. He was pretty old already when I was born, but he's always been the energetic type. Nearly ninety-three now, and he's hardly slowed down at all. He used to be a judge here in Palmer, you know. He's the one who got me interested in politics in the first place.'' He winked. ''I think he has great plans for me.''

Just then Angela Hockersmith strolled up and put an arm through Dwight's in a gesture of ownership no other woman could mistake. ''I hate to interrupt your chat,'' she said, looking at Jackie with hooded eyes, ''but Dwight has to go do the mingling thing. You know how it is in politics.''

''No,'' said Jackie, ''but I can guess.'' She was pretty sure Angela hadn't hated interrupting at all. She gave them a little wave of the hand as Angela hauled Dwight away to a group of suits in a far corner. She had great plans for Dwight too, evidently.

And imagine her thinking Jackie would be interested in her husband in the first place! Jackie bristled. Dwight Hockersmith wasn't bad looking in an earnest young politician sort of way, but there was something weak about him, Jackie had already decided. Perhaps it was too soon to make such a snap judgment, but she had a feeling he wasn't the kind of man who made his own decisions about things, and that sort of man wasn't appealing to her in the least.

''The next mayor of Palmer,'' said a voice just behind her. Jackie turned to see Olin Oliver, a self-satisfied expression on his bland, pleasant face as he nodded toward the retreating figure of Dwight Hockersmith across the room.

''I appreciate your enthusiasm, Olin, but from what I can

tell, it never seems to matter who's mayor of Palmer,'' Jackie replied. "We can keep right on buying a new cow every four years, but the bull in this town goes on forever."

"Dwight's different," said Olin. "A real reformer." He ran a hand through thinning dark hair and adjusted his tie. Olin was always fussing with himself, an unfortunate habit in the age of mass media that had done nothing for his brief political career. After conceding a handful of local elections he had gotten out of politics before being branded a total loser, and had secured a job teaching Poli Sci at Rodgers University shortly after Jackie had returned here from the prosaic little suburb of Kingswood, Ohio and secured an instructor's position in the R.U. Communications Department. They weren't friends—barely acquaintances, even— but she often caught him looking at her with a sort of sad longing. Unfortunately for Olin, romantic desperation really doesn't make people more attractive.

"I hope you're right," she said. I'm still pretty cynical about it, but I have to admit this town could use some fresh blood in City Hall. I'd probably vote for him just to see Jane out of a job."

"Just so you vote for him," said Olin. "He's asked me to be his campaign manager," he confided, leaning closer. "I'm thinking about accepting, but only if I can do it without giving up my day job, of course."

"Of course."

"Well, I'd better go do that mingling thing," said Olin with an apologetic shrug.

"Yeah, I know how it is in politics," said Jackie with a smile. She congratulated herself ruefully. She was getting good at this. Frightening thought.

She caught sight of Marcella Jacobs and raised a hand in greeting. Marcella walked over and greeted her with an eager smile. "So is this going to be some campaign, or what?"

"The fact that anyone's opposing Jane is cause for some

excitement, I guess. I don't know if Olin's man has what it takes to unseat her, though.''

"Oh, I don't care who wins, especially," said Marcella, "but it's going to get dirty, and when that happens it's worth a lot of ink. I have it from an unimpeachable source that Jane's got detectives trying to dig up dirt on Dwight, and I'd bet a weekend in New York he's doing exactly the same thing to her. He is if he has a brain, anyhow. As soon as one of them gets their hands on a piece of scandal, no matter how small, I want to be there to reap the rewards. You know how it is in the news business," she added.

"I know I'm glad I never had the urge to run for office," said Jackie. "When did we start expecting officeholders to be perfect? I think I wasn't paying attention."

"If you want to run for assistant dogcatcher these days, you'd better not have used crib notes in your kindergarten alphabet finals," Marcella agreed. "I'm glad I'm a reporter—nobody cares much what we do as long as we get the story. And if there's a story in Dwight Hockersmith," she said, looking across the room at the candidate standing with a little knot of Palmer's rich and influential people, "it's my job to get it." She gave Jackie a friendly pat on the arm and walked off.

Jackie sighed wearily. This was even drearier than she had anticipated, and she hoped her mother would agree to leaving early. She felt a headache coming on.

Frances sidled up to her with a plate of food and a glass of champagne. "The champagne's not half bad," she opined, "and the little meatballs are okay, but the baked brie is to die for."

"Have you ever thought of doing reception reviews for the Palmer Gazette?" Jackie asked her. "I could talk to Marcella Jacobs for you. She's right over there trying to get a good quote out of Dwight Hockersmith for the morning edition."

"Very funny, Jacqueline. Besides, I have my own contacts at the Gazette. It's not like being your mother is the only thing I'm known for in this town.''

That was certainly the truth, Jackie thought. ''I wouldn't dream of suggesting it. How long do you suppose we have to stick around here, anyway?''

''At least until I've had another go at the brie,'' said Frances, walking off toward the food table.

CHAPTER 4

Jake panted with pleasure and opened his mouth wide in a big shepherd grin, tongue lolling. The old woman's small, slender hand patted him between the ears. "What a good, sweet doggie you are," she crooned. "You're so beautiful!" She looked up at Frances. "Have I met him before?"

"No," Frances assured her, "this is the first time Jake has been here to visit you. He's my daughter's dog. This is my daughter, Jackie. You haven't met her, either."

The woman held out a quivering hand to Jackie. She looked younger than her eighty-two years, with a pixie face and pale, translucent skin beneath a cloud of pure white hair. She was seated in a hospital wheelchair, neatly dressed in a pink and blue sprigged cotton dress with a crisp white collar. "I'm Winnie," she said, "Winnie Swann. I'm married to Franklin Swann. He's a bank robber."

"Uh, pleased to meet you, Mrs. Swann," Jackie replied, taken aback somewhat. It wasn't every day that she heard such an unusual introduction.

A motherly nurse in a sky-blue uniform with a white tag that read 'Noreen Smith' clucked at Winnie as she handed her a fluted paper cup of water and another holding a tiny blue pill. "Franklin wasn't a bank robber, Winnie—he was an accountant. I don't know where you get these crazy ideas.'' She smiled indulgently at the old woman and shook her head.

Winnie looked up at Noreen sorrowfully. ''Oh, that's right,'' she said softly, ''Franklin's dead. Why do you suppose I can never seem to remember that?''

''Well, you have a bit of a problem with your memory, hon,'' Noreen replied gently. ''Now take that pill for me, that's it, dear.''

''It's too bad Mr. Swann didn't rob a bank or two,'' Noreen whispered to Jackie and Frances. ''Maybe poor Winnie wouldn't be flat broke now.'' She made a note on Winnie's chart and hung it over the end of the bed. Then she crumpled the little paper cups, tossed them into a wastebasket, and left the room.

Jake laid his head in Winnie's lap and abandoned himself to her petting and crooning with a look of utter contentment. Jackie took hold of Frances' sleeve and pulled her to the other side of the bed. She lowered her voice to a near-whisper. ''How long does she have before they . . .''

''End of the month,'' said Frances. ''If they had a promise of more money, they could let her ride for a while, but Franklin retired about twenty-five years ago. No one seems to know where his money came from after that. Apparently he had no retirement plan, and the Social Security's not enough to pay her keep here.''

''What about their house? Can she sell it?''

''No, there's supposedly some problem with Franklin's will. I don't know what that's all about.'' Frances shook her head impatiently. ''There's no more money in the bank account, and when they contacted Franklin's children, they refused to take responsibility.''

''For their own mother?'' Jackie was horrified.

''Oh, for God's sake, I'm not their mother,'' said Winnie.

Jackie jumped, embarrassed at having been overheard.

She started to apologize, but Winnie continued on as though she hadn't noticed.

"Dalton and Claire are Franklin's children from his first marriage. Franklin left his wife to marry me, you know. They've never forgiven me for that, not that I give a fig. Dalton and Claire's mother! What a fate *that* would have been. If I'd given birth to them, I'd probably have drowned them before they were three days old."

Jackie and Frances regarded one another with surprise. Winnie might be confused about the present sometimes, but she seemed to have a clear view of the past, and plenty of strong opinions of her own, at least where Franklin Swann's offspring were concerned.

Noreen poked her head back inside the doorway. "Maybe you two would like to take Winnie for a walk outside," she suggested. "We've got lots of nice paved paths out back—almost like regular little nature trails if you sort of ignore the concrete. I'll send someone in to straighten her room while she's out."

"It's been a long time since I've walked a dog," said Winnie. "At least I'm pretty sure it has. I think that would be very nice."

"Well, that settles it," said Jackie. She clipped the leather lead onto Jake's collar and slipped the looped end over Winnie's hand. "We're going for a stroll. Hang on tight, now."

Jake led the odd little procession out of the sliding glass doors at the rear of the convalescent home and down a wide concrete ramp toward a meandering path that wound around through numerous shrubs and trees that some astute landscaper had allowed to remain when the rest of the grounds were manicured into conformity with every boring hospital lawn in North America.

Spring was coming on strong and wildflowers were starting to push up here and there—the early ones, like crocuses and daffodils—even though the threat of frost would not be entirely over for weeks yet here in the midwest. Jackie had long since learned about the fickleness of local weather, and not to put her sweaters away until after Memorial Day.

Frances pushed Winnie's chair along the path and kept up a running commentary about their surroundings, while Jackie kept an eye on Jake. She was pretty sure he had the good sense not to take off chasing a rabbit or something while the old woman had his lead, but this was probably not a circumstance he would have encountered in his former life as a police dog. To her great pride, he walked calmly and slowly, never even tugging on his end of the lead no matter how slowly they progressed. He looked at his mistress as though for the approval that was due him for this sterling performance. Jackie obliged him with a pat on his broad shoulders. "Good boy, Jake," she said.

"Franklin so loved the springtime," Winnie sighed as they strolled along. "He'd work in the garden on weekend mornings, then he'd start fixing things around the house. Painting and plastering. Plastering and painting. Fixing the floors. The house kept getting older, just like us, but Franklin kept right up with it, especially after he retired."

"How lucky for you," Jackie observed. "A lot of men can't be bothered with home improvements. They're too busy watching sports all weekend while the house falls down around their ears."

"Well, not my Franklin," Winnie recalled fondly. "The only thing he really liked to do besides working on the house was to go off for one of those three-day trips of his to Chicago or Indianapolis or Pittsburgh. He went every spring and fall. I didn't go with him—those were his trips, to enjoy all by himself. Besides, he always came back with a lovely present for me."

She talked on for a few more minutes about Franklin, but she didn't bring up the subject of bank robbery. Jackie was curious about why Winnie should think her husband was a career criminal, but she could think of no graceful way to bring the subject back up.

After a leisurely turn around the grounds, they headed back for the main building. An aide helped Winnie out of her dress and into a brightly patterned nightgown, and helped her into bed for her afternoon nap. Jake sat at attention, following every motion with his eyes as if making sure that everything was done well enough to pass his personal inspection.

"You take it easy, Winnie," Frances told the old woman. "I'll be back on Thursday."

"I'll try to remember," Winnie sighed. "Will you bring Jake with you?"

"Well, I can't bring him every time," said Frances, "but I'm sure he can come back soon."

"It was nice meeting you, Winnie," said Jackie. She held out her hand and the old woman shook it firmly. "I'll bring Jake back to visit you next week."

Winnie smiled and closed her eyes. Jackie and Frances tiptoed to the door, with Jake bringing up the rear.

"And I've got lots and lots of money," Winnie said from behind them just as they reached the doorway. "It's just that I don't know where it is. Franklin knew, but he died without telling me. If I didn't love him so much, I'd be mad as hell about that. I think maybe I am anyway."

Jackie and Frances walked back over to the side of Winnie's bed. "Noreen says there's no more money in your bank account, Winnie," Frances told the old woman as gently as possible.

"Oh, not in the bank, no!" Winnie snorted in derision. "If anyone knew about the shortcomings of banks, it was Franklin. He'd never trust any significant amount of money to a bank!"

"If Franklin didn't put the money in the bank, where do you think he put it?" asked Jackie.

"I'm certain it's somewhere in the house," Winnie said.

"I have a key, you know. I'm sure I do somewhere around here. Look in that chest of drawers, there's a dear." Frances walked over to the chest of drawers under the window, and began to look through Winnie's clothing and possessions.

On top of the chest was a white linen dresser scarf embroidered with yellow and blue and lavender flowers tied up in a broad pink embroidered ribbon, and on top of that was a collection of framed photographs. Jackie walked closer and examined them. "Are these pictures of you and Franklin?" she asked Winnie.

"Yes. Wasn't he handsome?"

The earliest photos were of Franklin—decidedly handsome, with gentle eyes and a mischievous smile—in an Army uniform, one arm around a petite and lovely young Winnie, leaning back on the fender of a late-1930s' vintage car. From Winnie's clothing, Jackie guessed that the picture had been taken during the Second World War.

"Did you meet during the war?" she asked.

"Yes, when Franklin was assigned to Fort Ord, out in California, before he shipped out to Europe. He was already married to Phyllis, of course."

"That would be Dalton and Claire's mother?"

"Yes, and they take after her, the two of them," said Winnie with a certain degree of vehemence. "Always out for what they can get. Dalton was forever pestering Franklin to sell the house and give him the money for one thing or another. Our house!" She shook her head. "I was always grateful the children never wanted to come live with us. I think it would have been the end of our relationship if I'd had to put up with them for more than an occasional visit."

"Winnie, I can't seem to find a key anywhere in these drawers," said Frances, coming up for air from the disarray of nightgowns and wrappers and undergarments. "Are you sure you have one here?"

"Oh, I might have hidden it, I suppose," Winnie sighed. "I'm afraid Franklin's caution tended to rub off on me after all those years. Just look a little harder, dear."

Jackie went back to the photographs. There were later snapshots of Franklin and Winnie with later-vintage automobiles, and some in front of a neat little house with young shade trees planted on either side of a roofed porch. They looked very happy together as the years went by. Jackie was curious about how Franklin had come to leave Phyllis and the children and marry Winnie, but it seemed impolite to ask.

"Gotcha!" Frances exclaimed. Jackie heard a slight clink of metal on wood, and Frances held up a small brass key on the end of a little gold ball chain. "It was under the liner paper."

"That's it!" Winnie crowed. "Now if you'll just go to the house," she said, "you can find the money where Franklin hid it."

"Do you have any idea where that may have been?" Jackie asked her.

Winnie shook her head. "It was always such a big damned secret," she said, exasperation plain in her voice. "He said it would be better if I didn't know too much. He said someday Lefty might be so afraid that what Franklin had hidden away wouldn't protect him anymore, and when that happened, he said, Lefty would come after him. He didn't want me involved."

"Lefty?" Jackie mouthed at her mother. It sounded like something out of one of the gangster movies she was preparing to show her film class later this week.

Frances shrugged. "Okay, Winnie, we're going. If there's money anywhere in your house, you can bet we'll find it."

Winnie patted Frances' hand. "I knew I could count on you," she said. "Just like I used to always count on Frank-

lin.'' Her eyes misted over with tears. ''Poor Franklin,''
she sighed. ''I miss him so.'' She looked straight into
Jackie's face with clear blue eyes. ''He was murdered, you
know.''

CHAPTER 5

Frances had argued for going in the dead of night, but Jackie thought it best if they entered Winnie's house in broad daylight, as though they had every right to be there, which they very nearly did. The house wasn't legally Winnie's any more, Noreen had told them, but no one else had shown up to lay claim to it, either. This way was less dramatic, true, but it was also less likely to cause undue suspicion among the neighbors.

"But what if whoever murdered Franklin is watching the house for some reason?" Frances had wanted to know when they had discussed their upcoming trip to Winnie's house the evening before.

"Oh, for pity's sake, Mother," Jackie had told her, "Winnie's husband wasn't murdered. That's just another of her fantasies."

Frances crossed her arms in a familiar pose of pure stubbornness. "We don't know that for a fact," she replied.

Jackie gave her mother a look.

"Well we don't," Frances insisted. "And if he *was* murdered, then how fortunate for everyone involved that you're already on the case!"

Jackie was more than a little out of patience with the way people she knew had begun to assume that whenever

31

a murder took place she and Jake ought to be somehow in the middle of the investigation. Her mother was one of the worst, but even the administration of Rodgers University had been known to call her in as an expert, simply because she had helped the police—specifically Detective Lieutenant Michael McGowan—on a few investigations.

Despite the fact that he had every reason to resent her involvement in so many local crimes, even Michael treated her like a fellow professional, though she never expected it from him or anyone on the Palmer Police Force. She didn't feel much like a detective, and she certainly didn't have a license, but she always seemed to be thrown into the middle of strange murder cases, and she was not entirely sure she liked it. It took up way too much of her time and energy, and seemed to encourage morbid interest from sensation-loving people like her mother.

"Let's get one thing perfectly straight," Jackie said, looking Frances sternly in the eye. "There's no murder here, and if there were a murder, I'd be the first person to walk away and leave the investigation to the police."

"Of course you would, dear," Frances said sweetly.

"I don't think I like your tone of voice, Mother," said Jackie, "but we'll overlook that for now. We're going to Winnie's house to look for some money because she wants us to. If there's no money there, which I strongly suspect will be the case, we'll lock the house back up and tell her we're sorry we couldn't help. What we're not going to do is investigate a murder, because there isn't any murder to investigate. And we're going in broad daylight like good, law-abiding citizens, because we're not breaking any laws."

Frances had been disappointed, of course, but finally agreed. They met at the house on Willow Street after Jackie's office hours were over, and after she had stopped by the house and picked up Jake. Peter had just arrived home and was hard at his homework, as promised, when Jackie arrived.

"I told you I'd do it as soon as I got home," he said, sounding more than a bit wounded when Jackie expressed her surprise at finding him bent over a hot textbook.

"I just hope you'll be so diligent when I'm gone," Jackie commented.

"But Mom, you told me if I let any of my grades slip, I'll have to give up karate until I get them back up again."

"That's what I said, all right." She had expected Peter's involvement with karate to be as short-lived as any pursuit that carried with it the onus of keeping his grades up and doing his homework, but she'd been happily surprised when that turned out not to be the case.

"Well, I don't want to have to stop and start again," Peter explained. "I'm going for my green belt exam right after the next report cards come out, and that would screw me up royally."

"You're right. It would. Well, don't let me stop you then. Have at it." She glanced over his shoulder at the math textbook that was open on his desk. "Anything you need help with?"

"Nah, it's not that hard, really. Besides, if I needed help with math, you'd be about the last person I'd ask."

"See? You're getting smarter already. That's my boy."

Jackie was glad karate had become an important part of Peter's life—it made things so much easier all the way around. "Well, I've got to meet Grandma," she said, searching the floor of Peter's room for the leather lead that she used to take the shepherd on outings. "I thought I'd take Jake along to give him a change of scenery. Have you seen his lead?"

Peter hadn't seen it, but she needn't have bothered—a few seconds later Jake came into the room wagging his tail and carrying the lead in his mouth, and ten minutes after that the two of them were cruising through the quiet old

neighborhood of wide, tree-lined streets and carefully
tended yards where Winnie Swann and her husband Franklin had lived before Winnie went to stay at Forest View.

Jackie recognized the house—older, but very well kept
up—from the photographs of Franklin and Winnie in Winnie's room at Forest View. The trees were a lot larger now,
and the yard was almost entirely shaded this time of day.
The yard had been recently mowed, Jackie noted, probably
by helpful neighbors, and Franklin's penchant for garden-
ing showed in the cheerful beds of flowers and shrubs that
lined the sidewalk and continued down both sides of the
house to the back fence.

The weeds were starting to get a hold in the spaces between the plants, for all that Franklin had carefully lined
the flower beds with bark chips, and Jackie wondered if she
should come by one day soon and pull them up before they
got any more unsightly. But if Winnie wasn't coming home
again, what difference did it make, really?

The houses on Willow Street were all at least sixty years
old—quaint by modern standards, but immensely appealing
to Jackie. She loved her converted townhouse in a former
industrial district of downtown Palmer, but she'd always
had a secret yen for one of these old houses designed before
the concept of three-bedroom ranch-style dwellings in the
suburbs were a gleam in some demented architect's eye.
Of course she'd always dreamed of living in a Victorian
mansion, and in a log cabin in the mountains, too. You
can't have everything, she reminded herself, but there's no
harm in wishing.

Frances's car was pulled up to the curb outside, and as
Jackie pulled in behind her she got out and closed the door.
"You're right on time, Jacqueline," she announced, as
though it was some rare occurrence that had to be remarked
upon.

Jackie bit back a defensive retort; although she'd spent
most of her life doing it, arguing with Frances Costello was

good practice for beating one's head against a brick wall, and she had no plans for that in the foreseeable future. Who needed it? "So are you, Mother," was what she said instead. "Shall we go inside?"

A plywood ramp—new since the latest of Winnie's photographs—led from the sidewalk to the raised stoop, and Jake bounded up it while Jackie and Frances took the steps. He beat them handily to the front door and stood there, tongue lolling out in a doggy smile, waiting for them.

Winnie had probably been in the wheelchair even before she went to Forest View, and this arrangement would have made it a lot easier to get in and out of the house, Jackie supposed. The front stoop was overhung by a steep roof to keep the rain off callers to the little house. A few leaves and catkins from the big trees littered the porch, and a few cobwebs had sprung up in its corners. The old house was beginning to show the first subtle signs of neglect.

Frances turned the key in the lock and pushed open the door. "Here we are," she said, sounding like someone getting ready to embark on a great adventure.

Jake muscled his way inside, forgetting his usual good manners, and trotted past the little entry hall into the living room. Jackie and Frances followed him inside.

The floor of the living room was polished hardwood with no rugs in evidence—another practical concession to Winnie's chair, no doubt. Everything was neat and clean except for a faint haze of dust that had begun to collect, probably since Franklin's death, which had been barely a month before.

Prints of jungle plants and tropical birds hung on the walls over a sturdy sofa and matching chairs that seemed to date back as far as the house and the neighborhood. A few bare spots showed in the dark green frizée fabric, but everything was spotlessly clean. There were even doilies on the backs and arms of the furniture. Jackie shook her head in wonder. No one had such things these days. Her own mother had never been one for frilly household accessories—when was the last time she'd even seen a doily, she wondered? She walked around the room, looking at the quaint furnishings.

Sunlight came in the south and east windows through ivory lace curtains, and added a warm glow to the little room. Shelves full of books lined one wall from the ceiling to the floor, and a television set topped with another of Winnie's crocheted dresser scarves and a grotesque nineteen-fifties' vintage T.V. lamp in the shape of a prowling panther occupied one corner. Jackie ran a finger over the panther's sleek ceramic flank, leaving a shiny black trail in the dust.

It was easy to imagine the house with Winnie sitting by the window crocheting doilies and embroidering dresser scarves while Franklin puttered around the place, fixing things that probably didn't need all that much fixing.

Not a bad way to spend one's old age, Jackie supposed, though it seemed unlikely that she'd be following Winnie's example herself. She had yet to find a man who was worth sticking to for five years, much less fifty-five, the way Winnie had to Franklin.

"I wonder where we should start?" she said, looking around.

"Well, if Winnie didn't know where the money was," Frances mused, "then it wouldn't have been in an easy sort of place, like drawers or cabinets. Franklin would have found a much more clever hiding place if he were trying to protect her from knowing too much."

"You're assuming there was any money in the first place," Jackie reminded her. "And that there was actually something for Franklin to protect Winnie from in the second place. I still don't think I'm convinced the money was ever here, much less that it's stolen loot from a bank robbery."

"Well, Winnie's convinced, and we promised her we'd

look for it. So let's get to it. I'll take the living room and kitchen, and you can look in the bedrooms and bathroom.''

"Jake!" Jackie yelled at her dog, "What do you think you're doing?"

After taking a long, slow look around the living room, Jake had taken to sniffing his way around the walls. He stopped just underneath a large silkscreen print of cockatoos in an avocado tree and whined.

"Jake, stop that!"

The whines turned to barks—loud, insistent ones. Jackie tried again to shush him, but he paid her no attention. Maybe Peter was right, and some obedience training was in order after all, she thought. Could this be the kind of behavior Jason Huckle had warned her to be on the lookout for?

"I'm going to put him out in the car," Jackie told her mother. "I can't figure out why he's acting like this." She took hold of Jake's collar and led him outside and down the sidewalk.

"Hello, there!"

Jackie jumped at the voice, which seemed to come from behind a hedge separating Winnie's yard from the one next to it. She looked in that direction, but saw only shrubbery.

A moment later a tall, gray-haired man came from between two boxwood shrubs, smiling and holding out his hand. "I'm Ed Woodrow, Franklin and Winnie's neighbor." Jake seemed totally unconcerned, greeting this stranger with his usual calm but alert aloofness. Then he turned his head back toward the front door of the house and stared intently.

"I'm Jackie Walsh. My mother and I are friends of Winnie's. She gave us a key and asked us to pick up some things for her." True enough, as far as it went. Jackie managed to feel less than terribly guilty for her white lie. "Are you the one who's been keeping up with the lawn?"

Ed Woodrow waved his hand as if to dismiss the importance of the task. "No trouble at all. I do our yard every Sunday afternoon like clockwork, then Claudia and I— that's my wife, Claudia—we sit out on the front porch and enjoy the smell of the cut grass. Been doing it for forty-seven years. I've been starting early here lately, and then bringing the mower over and trimming up this one, too. Terrible about Franklin." He shook his head sadly.

"Yes," Jackie agreed solemnly. "Terrible." She realized she had no idea how Franklin had died, and was grateful she hadn't been counted upon to. Winnie's next-door neighbor might have expected Jackie, who claimed to be Winnie's friend, to be a bit better informed.

"Nice dog," said Ed Woodrow, advancing his hand slowly toward Jake's head, then withdrawing it cautiously before he actually touched him.

"You can pet him if you like," Jackie assured him. "He's perfectly friendly."

Jake accepted a few gentle pats from the man, wagged his tail perfunctorily, then turned his head back toward the house and whined.

"Sometimes I wish we had a big dog like that," Ed Woodrow commented, nodding at Jake. "This is a pretty safe neighborhood, but we do have break-ins now and then. Why, just a few weeks ago, not long after Franklin died, someone tried to break into their house late one night. I heard the noise and came out here and they went running off. Too dark to see who it was."

"Winnie's lucky to have you for a neighbor," Jackie told him.

He smiled and blushed. "Well, we're always glad to do anything we can for Winnie." He gave Jackie a wave and ducked back through the boxwood to his own yard. "Just let me or Claudia know if there's anything we can help with," he called as he disappeared.

"Thanks," Jackie called back. "I will." She looked down at Jake, who was still staring at the house. "Come on, boy, she said, tugging on the lead. "I can't believe the way you acted in there. It's going to be timeout in the car for you." She led him down the flagstones to the sidewalk, and stopped to let a tiny, bent-over man shuffle slowly by. The man raised his hand, clad in a black glove, in a jaunty wave. When he'd gone past, Jackie opened the back door of the Blazer and let Jake in, then rolled both back windows halfway down for fresh air. "I'll try not to be too long," she said. "You just calm down a bit."

Jake barked at her as she turned and proceeded back up the sidewalk. She couldn't help wondering what had gotten into him, and was glad she had decided to take him to see Jason on Monday.

When she got back inside, Frances had the sofa upside down on the floor. She had removed the staples from the black gauzy fabric that was attached to the wooden frame, and was poking around in the springs. "Nothing in the furniture so far," she reported, "and no loose floorboards, either, at least not in here."

"There probably won't be, the way Franklin was always fixing things. I'll just go start on the bedrooms," said Jackie, already weary of the idea, and not yet begun on the real work.

An hour and a half later neither of them had found anything in Winnie Swann's house that didn't seem to belong there, and nothing that remotely resembled money. After exhausting the difficult places, Frances had taken out and replaced the contents of all the kitchen drawers and cabinets, looked for secret compartments, and been visibly disappointed when she didn't find any. She had even checked behind the appliances and inside the freezer, while Jackie had inspected mattresses and box springs, closet shelves and storage boxes, as well as every square inch of the tiny ceramic-tiled bathroom. Now they sat, exhausted, on the overstuffed sofa and wondered what to do next.

"What if the money's hidden somewhere besides in the

house?'' Frances offered. "What if it's out in the back yard?''

"What if there's no money in the first place?'' countered Jackie.

"You always come back to that,'' Frances complained. "Just because Winnie's a couple of sandwiches shy of a picnic, you think she's lying about the money.''

"Of course she's not lying, Mother, but she could easily be imagining it. I mean, come on—her husband the bank robber and murder victim? And who's this Lefty guy? Lefty? Oh, come on! It's just all too much like the movies.''

"Well, it might be just a bit farfetched, I'll grant you,'' Frances admitted, "but just because they make movies about farfetched events doesn't mean they never happen. And whether or not Franklin Swann ever robbed a bank, he could still have hidden money away somewhere. Maybe he was one of those eccentrics who keeps millions of dollars in the mattress.''

"Definitely not the mattress,'' Jackie groaned. "I looked.'' She leaned her head against the doily-bedecked sofa back and sighed with exhaustion. "Not anywhere else, either, if you ask me.''

"Now if Jake were one of those specially trained money-sniffing dogs like you see on the news on the television,'' said Frances, "I'll bet he could lead us right to it.''

"Yeah, right,'' said Jackie.

"Well, we did our best, Jacqueline, but I'm sorry to say it wasn't good enough. Winnie still doesn't have the money she needs to stay at Forest View.''

"I'm sorry, Mother. I know you don't want to see Winnie have to go to a state hospital, but there probably never was any money. Winnie's a sweet old dear, but well. . . .''

"Her antenna isn't picking up all the channels,'' Frances supplied. "I suppose you're right, dear. Thanks for trying, anyhow. I hate to give up, but I'm sure I don't know what else to do,'' said Frances. ''Maybe it'll come to me in a blinding flash or something.''

''Yeah,'' Jackie agreed wearily, ''we can always hope for a blinding flash.''

CHAPTER 6

Jackie pulled herself up from the sofa and picked up her car keys from the coffee table. ''Are you about ready to go? I should get home and unfreeze something for dinner.''

Frances got up with a sigh and locked the door locks again before they closed the door behind them and walked down the steps and out onto the sidewalk. She got into her old sedan and fastened her seat belt.

Well, thank God for one thing at least, Jackie thought to herself as she walked toward her car, and that was that all this make-believe criminal intrigue had turned out to be just that—make-believe. There was no bank robbery, no murder, and no tiresome and possibly dangerous case for her to become involved in just because perverse luck always seemed to put her in the middle of bizarre and downright weird situations. Now she could go home and fix dinner and get on with her life, and maybe this dose of reality had broken the streak. Maybe now this sort of thing would quit happening to her altogether. She smiled as she put the door key in the lock.

Jackie opened the door and was nearly bowled over by Jake, who leaped from the passenger seat and bounded up the sidewalk to stand, barking, at Winnie's front door.

"Jake! Not again, please!" She started after him, but was stopped short by a sudden thought.

"Mother, wait!" Jackie called as Frances started up her car. "What was that you said about Jake, back there in Winnie's house?"

"Damned if I remember now," said Frances. "Why?"

"You said, what if Jake could sniff money? Who says he can't? Michael told me he was trained to do several jobs, because the Palmer K-9 force was too small to let the dogs specialize. Look at him! He definitely smells something!" She walked back up to the house, where Jake was whining and scratching at the screen door. "Come on, Mother, let's give Jake a chance to show us what he's so excited about."

"Franklin probably hid some kibble in there somewhere," muttered Frances as she turned off her engine. She climbed out of the car and made her way up the walk to join Jackie on the stoop. She dug Winnie's key back out of her handbag and unlocked the locks again. "This had better be good, Jake," she said to the Shepherd. "I've had about enough disappointment for one day."

As soon as the door was open, Jake dashed inside and back over to the far living room wall where he had raised such a fuss before. He ran back and forth a couple of times, sniffing, then sat down and stared at the same spot he had chosen earlier. He turned toward his mistress, raising his ears and cocking his head as if to inquire why she was taking so long to check it out.

"What is it, Jake? What do you smell?" Jackie asked, crossing the room to join him.

Jake barked once, jumped up and put his front paws against the framed print of avocados and birds, and began to scratch at it.

"Jake, stop that! You're going to scratch the frame!" Jackie pulled Jake down by his collar and took him a few feet away from the wall. "Stay!" she commanded. She went back to the print and tried to straighten the heavy wooden frame, but as she pulled against the wire hanger the nail that had held the picture in place came loose from the wall, bringing a chunk of plaster with it, and she had to scramble to keep from dropping the whole thing on her foot.

Jake leaped up from his spot and came back over to Jackie and the damaged wall. He pawed and scratched at the exposed plaster. Larger chunks began to fall away, dropping onto the floor and exploding into white grit and powder on the hardwood.

"Jake, stop it! You're ruining it!" Jackie lunged for Jake's collar to pull him away again before he destroyed the entire wall, but before she could accomplish this she saw, behind the soft plaster, a gaping hole in the wall, and a big piece of clear plastic, and what looked like pieces of paper—hundreds, or perhaps thousands of pieces bundled together—sticking out of it. "Look!" she said to her mother. "There's something in here all right!"

Jake clawed at the plastic, and at the bundles of paper, and pulled at them with his teeth. Some of them came loose as they fell from the hole, spilling dozens of ten- and twenty-dollar bills onto the floor around their feet.

"Well I'll be damned," Frances said in a voice barely above a whisper. "I'll just be thoroughly damned."

Jackie looked back and forth between her dog and the wall and her mother, and wondered if her knees were about to give out.

CHAPTER 7

"So what do you think about Winnie's fantasies now?" Frances wanted to know. Jackie stared, open-mouthed, at the ruin of a wall in front of her, legs shaking, and held on to Jake's collar. "Good dog," she murmured absently. "Good dog." She patted Jake's head with her other hand. Jake looked extraordinarily pleased with himself.

She bent down to pick up a handful of bills from the floor. There was something strange about them, she thought, though she wasn't sure just what it was. She looked at one side of a twenty, then turned it over. The printing on the back side was gold, and the design was unfamiliar. Maybe this had been a wild goose chase after all. "Mother, I don't even think this is real money," she said to Frances. "Take a closer look at it."

Frances took the bill from Jackie's hand. "Well, I'll be," she said. "It must be an old goldback."

"A what?"

"A goldback."

"Is that anything like a greenback?"

"Well, they used to call ones, fives, and tens greenbacks because they were printed in green on the back, but twenty-dollar bills and higher were goldbacks. Like this one. 'Course I was just a child at the time, but your grandfather

Cooley saved a twenty-dollar bill when he turned in his old currency in 'twenty-eight, and he used to show it to us sometimes.''

"So this money was printed sometime before nineteen twenty-eight?''

"That's my guess,'' said Frances. "After that the paper money was all different, and they recalled the old stuff, and it wouldn't spend anymore. This is all just so much paper now, I suppose.''

"But it was real enough seventy years ago,'' said Jackie. "So the question seems to be . . .''

"What was Franklin Swann doing with it?'' Frances finished for her.

"Right—with so much of it? And why didn't he turn it in back in 1928?''

"Maybe,'' said Frances, and there was no mistaking the satisfied gleam in her eye, "because it was acquired in a bank robbery. And just maybe,'' she continued, warming to the idea rapidly, "if Franklin actually was a bank robber, then the idea of his also being murdered isn't as unlikely as you've been thinking it was.''

This time Jackie had no ready retort to her mother's morbid whimsy about robbery and murder. As much as she hated to admit it, she was curious. But this time, she promised herself solemnly, she'd go straight to the police and let them take care of it. Without her help. She said just that to her mother.

"Oh, piffle, Jacqueline,'' was Frances's response. "I can't count the number of times you've gotten right into the thick of cases that weren't half as fascinating as this one, just because someone you didn't even know got themselves killed.''

"Be fair, Mother,'' Jackie cautioned. "Sometimes it was someone I knew.''

"And now you have the chance to investigate a crime—maybe two crimes—and help an old woman who needs you, and the first thing you can think of is to dump the whole thing right into the laps of the police.''

"You say that as though there were a better choice," Jackie told her.

Frances sniffled loudly, for effect. "All I can say is, I hope this isn't the way you treat me when I'm sitting in a wheelchair in a convalescent home somewhere. 'Sorry, Mother. Let the police handle it.' ''

"Sorry, Mother, but that's their job. I'm a college instructor by trade, not a detective. I'd like to be able to help Winnie, but I'm afraid it's just not going to be possible."

"All I ask is that you think about it," said Frances, fixing Jackie with one of those looks mothers work so hard at perfecting, guaranteed to elicit loads of guilt.

"I'll think about it," Jackie promised.

It could be argued, Jackie supposed, that calling Michael McGowan in Hollywood and going straight to the police were not exactly the same thing, but maybe it was best to take this one step at a time, especially since she was having her doubts about how the police would proceed in the case of Winnie Swann's money.

Michael was still a police detective with the Palmer Police Department, but he was currently on leave of absence while he pursued his new-found scriptwriting career. Eventually, she supposed, he would come back to Palmer and back to police work. It seemed the natural choice for him. She wasn't exactly sure how she felt about it for herself, though.

Regardless of where the money had come from, Jackie persisted in thinking of it as Winnie's. It might have belonged to a bank once, she supposed, but if it was still worth anything, which she doubted, it was what Winnie needed to stay at Forest View. She had returned it to its place in the wall, then she and her mother had cleaned up the fallen plaster and replaced the print as best they could.

It would be better to leave the money there in the house, they thought, until they could figure out what else to do with it.

Luckily, she had the number to Michael's cellular phone, so she didn't have to chase him from place to place all over Los Angeles County. He even seemed pleased to hear her voice. "To what do I owe the pleasure?" he asked, and any sarcasm Jackie could detect was slight indeed.

"Less pleasure than it is business, I'm afraid, Michael."

"Police business or television business? As if I couldn't guess. You haven't gotten yourself mixed up in another murder, have you?"

Jackie could tell he was joking, at least partly. She wondered if his smile would fade when he learned the truth. Well, no matter. She couldn't run her life by Michael McGowan's reactions, not that she ever had, she hastened to reassure herself. "More on the police side, I guess. Would you mind answering a hypothetical question?" she asked him.

"I guess not." His voice sounded a bit troubled now. "Shoot."

"Suppose someone found a large amount of money?"

There was a brief silence on the other end of the line. "That's your question?"

"Well, it's the beginning of it."

"Okay. The beginning of my answer is that the person who found it should turn it over to the police."

"But then wouldn't it be stuck away somewhere not doing anyone any good?"

"Well, the police would check to see whether the money might be evidence in a crime, of course. If it wasn't, and if the rightful owner couldn't be found, it would revert to the person who found it."

"Right away?"

"There'd be a waiting period. Of course if it was evidence of some sort, then the money might be tied up until the case came to court. That could take a while, I guess.''

"What if the person who found it was already pretty sure about the crime part?"

"Jackie, this question of yours is getting less and less hypothetical. You're sure you're not involved in something . . .''

"Criminal?" She thought about that for a moment. "No, I don't think so.''

"You don't *think* so? You found some money and you're pretty sure it's linked to a crime and you haven't turned it in, and you don't *think* so?''

"Calm down, Michael, and let's keep this hypothetical a while longer. I never said I found any money. I simply asked you what would happen if someone did.''

"Well, I think a hypothetical arrest for withholding evidence might be in order, or perhaps a hypothetical jail term for obstructing justice." He was definitely not smiling now, though she thought he was doing a pretty good job of controlling himself.

"Suppose the crime happened a long, long time ago— way beyond any statute of limitations.''

"Depends on the crime. If a homicide were involved, there'd be no statute of limitations.''

"And if the money was stolen?''

"Legally it'd still belong to whoever it was stolen from. If the rightful owner couldn't be located after a certain length of time, the finder might be able to establish a right of salvage and claim the money. Would you just possibly like to fill me in on what the hell's going on?''

"Not really. And besides, who said there was anything going on? I certainly didn't.''

"Oh, come on, Jackie. This is Michael, remember? I know you pretty well.''

He had her there. At one time, and not all that long ago, she and Michael had been as close as two people can be. It could be argued that he knew her as well as anyone did, and she'd never thought of herself as being all that easy to know. "If you know me that well, then you ought to know you can trust me," she countered. "You know I'm not going to do anything criminal—I've got Peter to think about."

"How is Peter, by the way?"

Now it was Jackie's turn to smile. Michael and Peter had grown quite fond of one another during the course of Michael and Jackie's relationship. Michael had made a pretty good male role model for Peter—a far better one than his self-centered, upwardly mobile father ever had, and Peter had made no effort to hide the fact that he wouldn't half mind having Michael around on a permanent basis. Of course, Jackie had once had similar thoughts herself, but that was all in the past.

Peter had been thrown for a loop by the breakup, leading to all sorts of behavior problems that were only now beginning to smooth themselves out. That was more her fault than Michael's, and she'd frequently felt more than a little guilty about it. "You wouldn't recognize him," she said. "He's four inches taller, has muscles where the fat used to be, and he's almost human."

"I've always thought Peter was a great kid," Michael said. "I miss him."

"I know." Jackie felt her voice starting to fail her. She took a couple of deep breaths before going on, and blinked back the tears that were threatening to blur her vision. "He misses you, too. You two were good for one another."

She heard Michael sigh into the phone. "You and I were pretty good too, once."

"Yes, we were," she agreed. "Once."

Michael hadn't told Jackie anything she hadn't already suspected about the money hidden in Winnie Swann's living room wall, presumably by her late husband, Franklin. If there had been a crime, and despite her continued denials to her mother, it seemed pretty likely to her that there had been, then the money should go directly to the police as evidence. She knew exactly what she had to do, she told herself firmly as she dialed her mother's number.

Frances Costello had her own ideas on that. "You must be out of your mind if you think I'm going to let you take that money to the police, Jacqueline Shannon Costello!"

Like most mothers of Jackie's experience, Frances only used her child's full and complete name under the most extreme circumstances, like her announcement of her engagement to Cooper Walsh, or the time, at seven years of age, when she broke an heirloom relish bowl. Jackie braced herself for an argument that seemed lost from the beginning.

"Withholding evidence from the police is a crime, Mother. I have that on very good authority." She outlined what Michael had told her about the hypothetical money.

"We don't even know it's evidence," Frances countered. "You said yourself there was no proof a crime had been committed in the first place. You can't have it both ways, you know. Either there was a crime, or there wasn't one."

Frances had an absolute genius for making people eat their words, and she practiced it on Jackie frequently. "Well, I don't know about you, Mother, but I'm not going to stroll into every bank in the midwest and ask if they were held up seventy years ago and whether the money is still missing."

"It's not very likely anyone at a bank would even have that information," said Frances, "but luckily or otherwise, there's one American institution that never forgets. Newspapers."

It was never easy for Jackie to admit her mother might actually be right about something, particularly something they'd just been arguing about, but there it was, and she was an adult, after all, or supposed to be. "You're right," she said, and it barely hurt at all, really. "Of course.

There'll be microfilm records in the library downtown. I've got a class in an hour, but I'll go right down there afterwards.''

"Not by yourself, you won't," Frances assured her. "I'm damned if you're going to have all the fun."

"Okay," Jackie conceded. "I'll meet you at the downtown branch of the Palmer City Library a few minutes after three. And Mother?"

"Yes, darling daughter?"

"Don't you dare do anything until I get there."

There was a disconcerting silence from Frances' end of the phone line.

"Promise me."

"Oh, good heavens, I'm not old enough for you to pull this role-reversal business. Stop acting like my mother, Jacqueline."

This time the silence was on Jackie's end.

"Oh, all right," Frances grumbled. "I promise. Don't be late, though."

CHAPTER 8

"The popularity of the gangster films of the nineteen-thirties was Depression-era American society's way of thumbing its nose at the so-called American Dream—the Horatio Alger myth of poor-but-honest-boy makes good.'' Jackie looked out over the faces of her Tuesday afternoon Film and Society class, which met in the basement of the Longacre Communications Arts Center on the Rodgers University campus.

Despite the beautiful spring weather outside, barely visible as rays of sunshine through the small windows high up on the east wall, the majority of the students were actually awake and listening to her lecture. "After all,'' she said, "the movies were cheap entertainment, and all but the very poorest people could afford to go. Hollywood did very well by itself during those years catering to people who in most cases had very little disposable income. No matter how little money they have, people have a need for entertainment, and when times are hard, that need seems to increase. We hadn't yet been blessed with television . . .''— the class laughed, catching her sarcastic tone—"so people went out to the movies. A lot.''

Jackie riffled through her index cards full of barely legible lecture notes and found her next point. "By the time the Depression struck the U.S., the European immigrants who had flocked to America by the millions in the eighteen-nineties were mostly older people with children and grand-children. Those younger generations had an entirely different take on what life in the Promised Land was really like than their parents had had back home, looking across the Atlantic with longing for a better life. The American Dream had failed their parents, and it was failing them, too." Her students could probably relate to that, thought Jackie. Every generation found itself failed in some way, even one as prosperous as this one. Poverty and discrimination were still everywhere, though perhaps a bit harder to find on the campus of a private university than in other, less affluent places you could think of.

"No matter where you went in those days," Jackie continued, "you could see vast numbers of hungry, unemployed people. They were all over the streets, standing in line for a day's work for fifty cents or a dollar, when they could get it, or riding the rails like you saw recently in *Sullivan's Travels*. They were in broken down vehicles on the sides of the highways of America with all their possessions loaded on old cars and trucks, like you saw in *The Grapes of Wrath*. It was obvious that something was very wrong with the dream the parents and grandparents of this new American generation had given up everything to come here and find."

Jackie's own grandparents on both sides had come to America from Ireland in the nineteenth century—her mother's people because they had been among the lucky few with enough money to escape the worst of the Irish famine of the 1840s and her father's a bit later in the century, fleeing the effects of English rule in the northern counties. She was no stranger to stories of immigrant hardships and the awful, grinding poverty of the Great Depression. There had been economic hard times for a lot of people since then, but she'd been lucky enough to escape them.

"Now it's the thirties, and here comes Hollywood with the gangster film," she continued. "Now we have the poor-but-*dis*honest-boy making good. It wasn't just a flight of fancy on Hollywood's part—film always reflects to some extent the society in which it exists, which is why I can give this class, and you can get academic credit for sitting here watching movies." A brief ripple of laughter from the class.

"After the gangster films had their day, there was a certain amount of pressure on the entertainment industry to stop glamorizing crime and criminals and give America some films based on solid, law-abiding values."

"Of course that couldn't happen today," she added, straight-faced. The students laughed again.

"Those were the G-Man films of the forties, but I won't take up your time showing any of them, because they weren't any good, and they all went down to well-deserved obscurity. Art doesn't work that way, thankfully. Art can reflect political realities, but when it bows to political pressure, it isn't art any more. In the case of these films it could barely be called craft."

"Yeah, but tell us what you really think, Ms. Walsh," said John McBride, one of her brighter students. "Did you like them?"

"*So*," Jackie went on, giving John McBride a mock-withering look, "back to the gangster films. They were fiction, but like all myth—all fiction of any kind, all art of any kind—they took their heart from fact. They drew on a common American story about a common American guy that everyone was at least somewhat familiar with—the son or grandson of immigrants to whom all avenues of advancement seem closed off except that of crime.

"In this America, this land of so-called unlimited opportunity that many folks could never quite reach, a country that had opened its doors but closed its heart to many of these immigrants, a criminal could be a king of sorts. Many

were felt to be heroes of the common people, partly because
they came from those same transplanted, disadvantaged
roots, and partly by virtue of being on the wrong side of
the law. The man and woman on the street at that time
largely thought of the law as being at best biased, and at
worst corrupt, a tool of the rich designed to keep them
down.''

"Well, there's one thing that hasn't changed much,"
piped up a voice from the back of the room. Marti Bern-
stein, this time—the last tie-dyed, Rasta-haired hippie in
Palmer, Ohio, and the oldest and longest-running professional student at Rodgers University.

Jackie smiled. "For what it's worth, Marti, I agree with
you, but for a deeper discussion than this one you'll have
to take Sociology, and I think you've already got a degree
in that." The bell sounded, ending the lecture. "Film lab
tomorrow," Jackie reminded them, raising her voice to be
heard over the scraping of fifty textbooks against fifty
desks, and the shuffling of a hundred feet. "*Public Enemy*
and *Little Caesar*. Showtime is 9 A.M. sharp. Be there."

The students left the room in the usual chaotic rush of
bodies eager to be anywhere on a lovely spring day but
inside a lecture hall. Jackie could certainly understand that,
but before she could think about guilty pleasures like rest
or relaxation, she had to drive over to the city library and
pore over some seventy-year-old newspaper articles. She
really must remind herself not to let her mother, or anyone
else, ever drag her into another situation like this. She
called home and left a message for Peter, telling him she'd
be home in time for supper, and reminding him to do his
homework.

"Mother, I'm getting a headache from trying to read all
this tiny little type, and I still haven't found anything about
a bank robbery. Maybe it didn't even happen around here.
Are we going to check every paper in the country?''

"Stop whining, Jacqueline. We'll start here and if we come up dry we'll work our way out to other cities nearby. Just concentrate on the headlines—if someone robbed a bank, it'd be in large type on the front page. Anyhow, you probably just need reading glasses."

Jackie bristled at the suggestion. "I'm thirty-eight years old, Mother. I don't need any such thing. Pass me another microfiche."

It was another half-hour, countless little rectangles of microfilm, and one full-blown headache later when Jackie finally spotted the headline they'd been looking for. "FIRST CENTRAL BANK ROBBED!" the banner screamed. "Daring Daylight Raid Nets $150,000!" declared a subhead, and the article underneath went on to tell how three masked men had walked into the First Central Bank of Palmer, Ohio near closing time on June 17, a Friday, and walked out with what in 1927 dollars was a staggering amount of money.

"Well, now at least there's no debate over whether there actually was a bank robbery shortly before the currency was recalled," said Frances, reading the article with undisguised enthusiasm.

"But we still don't know if Franklin Swann was involved, or whether the money we found is connected," Jackie argued. "We've found an interesting possible link, but we haven't actually proved anything."

"But we know there's thousands of dollars hidden in the walls of his house, and we know he never went to prison for robbery," said Frances. "If the money were legitimate, why would Franklin have hidden it, and why wouldn't he have turned it in for new currency back in twenty-eight? As far as I'm concerned, that means the existence of that money is the best proof we'll probably ever have."

"I hate to admit it, of course, but you just might possibly be right," said Jackie.

"Well, don't break your neck trying to avoid admitting it," her mother cautioned.

"Oh, here's something interesting," said Jackie, glancing down the body of the article for any other information that might be useful. "It says one of the robbers was shot in the hand by a bank guard. Apparently it looked like a serious wound, and he seems to have lost a lot of blood, but by the time the article was written, no one had checked into a hospital anywhere in Ohio or any neighboring state for a gunshot wound in the hand."

"Let's check the papers for the next week or so for follow-up stories," said Frances. "Maybe there were further developments in the case." She checked the dates on a microfiche on her stack, slipped it out of its envelope, and inserted it into the viewer. Bank robbery stories followed for the next several weeks, slowly making their way off the front page and onto the second, third, fourth, and so on, as leads in the case dried up and the daring daylight bank robbers were never apprehended.

"Wait a minute," said Jackie, looking up from her reading. "There is no First Central Bank in Palmer. I've never heard of a bank by that name."

"A lot of banks went under in 1929," said Frances. "That was probably one of them."

"Then if there's no bank to claim ownership of the money," Jackie suggested, "it could be Winnie's, free and clear."

"Except for the tiny matter of evidence," Frances commented drily.

"Yeah, except for that. Well, none of the stories say anything about a homicide committed during the robbery, so it's likely that the statute of limitations applies in this case. Maybe Winnie owns the money after all."

"I wonder if it counts if the man who was shot in the hand died later?" Frances said. "I mean he could have, from loss of blood, couldn't he? Wouldn't that be a homicide just the same as if one of the robbers had killed some-one?''

''I guess so,'' Jackie replied, ''though I'm not sure how that would affect the statute of limitations. So there were three men,'' Jackie mused. ''I wonder who the other two were?''

''Maybe Winnie knows,'' Frances suggested.

CHAPTER 9

"Well, I know one of them was named Lefty," Winnie supplied when they visited her later that afternoon at Forest View, "but I don't know his real name. Lefty didn't trust Franklin to keep his secrets, and Franklin was always a little bit afraid of what Lefty might do, but he said he had something on him, and that should keep him safe." She seemed to focus on Jackie for the first time since they'd arrived ten minutes before. "Aren't you Florence Allred's daughter?"

"I'm Frances Costello's daughter," Jackie reminded her. "I visited you the other day. I brought my dog."

"Oh, I remember the dog!" Winnie exclaimed, clapping her hands. "We went for a walk, didn't we?"

"That's right. Now Franklin had something on Lefty?" Jackie prompted, "Some evidence?"

"He'd never tell me. Don't think I wasn't curious, but Franklin had a way of turning my curiosity aside, especially when it came to Lefty. After a while I learned not to ask."

Winnie had been relieved to hear that the money had been found, but was a little unclear on why it wasn't any good any more. Jackie decided it really didn't matter whether or not she could remember that the currency hidden in her wall by her late husband was outdated by seventy years, as long as they could establish her legal right to it, and maybe arrange for some more of it to be sold off piece-meal to cover her living expenses. Time was running out for Winnie at Forest View without some help that neither she nor Frances had the ready cash to offer.

"You mentioned that Franklin was afraid Lefty might come after you," Jackie continued. "Does this mean he might still be alive?"

"Well, he was alive when Franklin was," said Winnie, but right now I can't remember just when that was."

"Franklin died about a month ago," Frances supplied. "And you think Lefty was alive then?"

"Oh, absolutely," Winnie averred, nodding her head slowly. "Franklin was fussing about Lefty the last time he visited me, though I'm not sure exactly when that was."

"Well, Noreen says he visited every day," so it probably would have been just before the accident," Jackie told her.

"It was no accident," said Winnie solemnly. "Franklin was murdered."

So they were back to that again. Jackie had already quizzed Noreen, the day nurse on Winnie's wing, about the circumstances surrounding Franklin Swann's death, and they'd been much more mundane than poor Winnie's im-aginings. Apparently he'd climbed up on a ladder to fix something on his roof, and the ladder had slipped. Franklin had fallen to his death on the cement sidewalk in front of his house. It had been ruled a clear-cut case of accidental death.

Frances had been disappointed to learn the pedestrian manner of Franklin's death—murder was ever so much more appealing to her mother, Jackie noted to herself, but Frances was bearing up well as long as there was the mys-tery of the seventy-year-old bank robbery still to be solved, as well as the mystery of how to keep Winnie Swann from being evicted from her comfy home at Forest View. Jackie wondered if she ought to retire from the accidental detective business and leave all future investigations to her mother.

"How about the third man?" Frances was asking the old woman.

Winnie gave this some serious thought. "Barney Dorf-meier," she proclaimed after some time. "He was Frank-lin's best friend in college. They were friends for more than seventy years."

"Do you think he's still alive?"

"I think so," said Winnie. "I just can't be sure. I can remember Barney so well, you know, from the old days. He used to come over to the house for dinner sometimes. I think he was still coming over after I had to come here, but I don't remember when that was." Her forehead wrin-kled with effort as she tried to recall.

"That's not really important, Winnie," Jackie assured her. "Don't worry about it."

"Barney would come to visit," Winnie continued, "and I'd cook dinner, and afterwards the two of them would go out to the backyard and smoke a cigar and talk about the old days. A lovely man. He married a local girl and had three children, but she died some years ago and he went to live with his daughter. No, it was his granddaughter. What was her name? Elizabeth Batcheler. Now I remember." She looked pleased for a moment, then apologetic again. "I just can't seem to remember whether he's still alive or not."

Jackie marveled at the detail of Winnie's long-term memories, especially when compared to how little she could recall of the most recent events. "Well, don't worry about it," said Jackie. "We should be able to find that out for ourselves with a little effort."

"Thank you, dear," said Winnie, patting Jackie's hand. "That takes a load off my mind. It's so tiring trying to keep things straight anymore."

Jackie could certainly sympathize with that, and *her*

memory was pretty nearly perfect. It was the rest of her life that wouldn't stay uncomplicated.

"So, who do you think would have wanted Franklin dead?" Frances asked Winnie.

"Mother, don't encourage this," Jackie warned.

"Why, Lefty, of course," Winnie snorted. "Franklin always told me that if he didn't die of natural causes, it'd be Lefty who killed him."

Jackie decided she wouldn't bring up the fact that Franklin's death had been an accident—she didn't feel like getting into that particular discussion with Winnie. "Yes, but who is Lefty?" she pressed. "What's his real name?"

"Franklin always said the less I knew. . . ."

"Yes, I know," Frances sighed wearily, "the safer you'd be."

"Why, that's *exactly* what he said." Winnie was clearly astounded. "Did you know Franklin?"

Frances patted the old woman's hand. "I'm beginning to feel like I did," she said.

"I wish we had a piece of that money," Jackie told her mother as they walked away from Forest View. "It seems to be Franklin's only retirement plan and Winnie's only hope for the future, and I'd like to take it to an expert and see what it's worth, if anything."

"I've still got Winnie's key," said Frances, taking the object in question from her pocket and holding it up, dangling on its little gold chain.

"I don't know, Mother," Jackie said, eyeing the key wistfully. "Even with a key, I'd feel like a criminal going back in there. The place is full of stolen money that we know about and haven't reported to the police." She looked at her mother, hoping for a shred of understanding.

Frances Costello was too practical for any such thing. "I wouldn't want you to think I haven't been giving the matter a lot of thought, Jacqueline," she said, "but it seems to me that since we know about the money and the robbery and we're not telling anyone, then we're criminals whether we go back to the house or not. If we go back, we can get a piece of the money and maybe we can be some help to Winnie. If we don't, we can't. And either way, neither of us seems to be in any hurry to go to the police about the whole thing.''

Jackie groaned. ''Don't remind me. I promised myself I would, and then I chickened out. I feel awful about it.''

''Just so you don't feel awful enough to do anything foolish, dear,'' said her mother, patting her arm in a nearly sympathetic sort of way.

Jackie decided to put aside, for now, any worries about her thriving criminal career. She checked the time on her wristwatch. ''Gosh, how time flies when you're having fun. I have to go home and fix dinner,'' she said. ''Care to join us?''

''Not tonight, dear, I've got Readers' Circle down at the bookstore, and I have to get home and read the last few chapters of *Lady Chatterley's Lover* before meeting time.''

''Readers' Circle has certainly gotten a lot more, um, interesting since I checked it out last,'' said Jackie, raising her eyebrow at her mother.

''Oh, all they needed was a gentle push in the right direction,'' said Frances modestly. ''I'll just be off now, dear. You be sure to give my love to my darling grandson.''

''I will, Mother.'' Jackie got into her Blazer and turned the key in the ignition, then sighed and rolled down the window. ''When should we go to Winnie's house again?''

''The sooner the better,'' said Frances. ''How about tomorrow morning, right after we check up on Mr. Barney Dorfmeier?''

''So did you go talk to Mr. Cusack today?'' Peter asked Jackie almost as soon as she walked in the door. He was actually done with his homework—Jackie checked to be absolutely sure—and digging through the refrigerator in search of food.

"Sorry. Not today, I'm afraid. Tomorrow for sure, though."

"Mom!" Peter gave the word an inflection only teen-agers can ever truly master, drawing it out to two long syllables freighted with disappointment and disbelief.

"I'm sorry, Peter. It's just that I've been helping your grandmother out with a problem a friend of hers is having, and it's kept me awfully busy. I haven't forgotten you want me to check into some training for Jake."

She didn't mention how much Jake's mood had seemed to improve since his discovery of a cache of outdated cur-rency in Winnie Swann's house. Jake had gone straight out to the backyard when they got home and started running back and forth, nosing his dog toys across the lawn and kicking his own rubber ball a few feet away, then running after it and kicking it again. She was sure he felt better, but that didn't mean he couldn't benefit from something else to keep him occupied.

"Will you go tomorrow morning, then? Please?" He managed not to whine, Jackie noted with satisfaction. That was one of the most welcome signs of improvement, as far as she was concerned.

"I've got a film lab from nine until eleven-thirty or so. Then I'm afraid I've got somewhere I have to be after that. Grandma's problem, again."

"Gee, Mom . . ."

Jackie had to admire her son's restraint. This time six months ago he'd have stomped off and slammed the door to his room. Well, if he could make the effort, so could she. "Actually, there's no reason it couldn't wait a couple of hours," she said. "I'll call your grandmother and tell her I'll meet her in the afternoon after my office hours at school. How's that?"

"And you'll go see Mr. Cusack right after the film lab thing? You promise?"

"I promise." She absorbed his skeptical look. "This time for sure," she added.

"Okay," Peter said. "I'm gonna hold you to it. Oh, and I checked the voice mail when I got home. Somebody called for you named, uh, Hoopersmith, or something like that."

"Hockersmith?"

"That could've been it. He's having a party tomorrow night at his house and he wanted to know if you and Grandma wanted to come. The address is over there on the notepad by the phone."

"Thanks, babe."

"It's probably not a real party or anything," Peter said. "Probably nothing interesting, I mean."

"You mean something *you'd* be interested in going to? No, I'm afraid it's one of those boring political things that spring up like toadstools in an election year. You'd be bored out of your skull. Maybe you'd like to have Isaac over and rent some movies. Your grandmother says there's a new Jackie Chan video out."

"Isaac's grounded for nearly flunking a math test," Peter informed her. "But if you want to rent the movie I'll just watch it by myself."

"You're sure you'll be all right on your own for a few hours?"

"Come on, Mom—I'm thirteen years old." His look told her just how ridiculous her question had been.

"Yeah. Practically an adult. Well, I just wanted to know if you minded, I guess."

"Throw in a Chuck Norris video and you can stay out all night," Peter assured her.

"Deal. *Lone Wolf McQuade* again?"

"*Code of Silence*," said Peter after a moment's thought.

"So why are you going to this party if it's going to be so boring, anyhow?" he asked.

"Because if I don't accept at least half of the social invitations I get, I tend to turn into a hermit who only goes from home to work and back home again," said Jackie. "It's worse when I'm not seeing anyone, like now. I've watched it happen to myself more than once. After a while I forget how to relate to anyone but you and Grandma."

Jackie gave a moment's thought to whether being a hermit might not be preferable to dealing with Angela Hockersmith again. "I wonder if I'm going to have to suffer through an evening at the Hockersmiths by myself," she mused. "Maybe I should ask Grandma if she's interested in going along."

"Will they have free food at this party?" Peter inquired.

"I imagine they will."

"Then Grandma'll want to go, all right," said Peter. "Absolutely no problem."

CHAPTER 10

The sight of Cusack Kennels, with its old buildings freshly painted and its new signs freshly hung, still brought an involuntary shiver to Jackie's spine. This place had a history for her, going back to when its original owner, Mel Sweeten, had been strangled with a choke chain in one of his own dog runs, shortly after she and Peter had returned to live in Palmer. And the unpleasantness hadn't ended there, either. Given a choice, she'd never have come back to this place in a million years, but Peter hadn't exactly given her a choice.

She had to admit, though, that it certainly looked a lot nicer now, and the slender, dark-haired man who was walking toward her car, dressed in faded blue jeans and an old chambray workshirt under a denim jacket, didn't look half bad himself.

The man waited for Jackie to get out of her car, then held out his hand. "I'm Tom Cusack," he said, gripping her hand firmly and smiling pleasantly. "You must be Jackie Walsh."

"That's me," Jackie said, returning the handshake and the smile.

"Peter told me you'd be coming by today." Dark blue

eyes regarded her out of a slightly weathered face under a head of dark hair starting to go a bit gray.

Jackie couldn't imagine she was the only person expected this afternoon, and wondered more than idly how Peter had told Tom Cusack to recognize her. "Peter must have told you to look for the frazzled-looking woman with the German Shepherd," she volunteered. Jake sat in the Blazer's passenger seat, favoring the stranger with his best coolly interested look, seeming to wait calmly for the part of the meeting that concerned him.

"Actually," said Tom Cusack with a little smile, "he told me to look for a beautiful woman with dark hair and a great figure."

"I'll kill him," she muttered, feeling a hot blush work its way up from the neck of her shirt to her hairline.

"Oh, don't be too hard on Peter. I recognized you right away, didn't I?" He walked closer to the car. "And this must be Jake," he said.

"That's him, all right. I thought I'd bring him by to get acquainted."

"Peter said you might want to give Jake some extra training. We can discuss that later, but if you don't mind leaving him in the car for just a few minutes, I'll show you around the place."

This didn't seem to be the time to remind her host that she had visited the business now known as Cusack Kennels more often than she would have liked, usually under circumstances far less pleasant than these. She could probably give *him* a tour. Well, no sense bringing up the past, she supposed. The kennels had a new coat of paint, a new owner, and a new attitude. She'd accept the tour and size up this hotshot dog trainer Peter seemed so taken with.

"Peter mentioned you might be interested in obedience training for Jake," Tom said as they strolled up a gravel driveway toward the kennel buildings. It was just past noon on Friday, and the weather, often a bit unpredictable this time of year, was holding nicely, with temperatures in the seventies. A slightly cooler breeze came through the stand of lovely old oaks on the hill above them as they walked.

"Jake's obedient enough most of the time," Jackie told him, remembering his recent insistence on exploring the contents of Winnie Swann's living room wall despite Jackie's strong objections, "but Peter's afraid he might be getting bored, and I have to admit he's been acting a little depressed lately, off and on."

"I remember now," said Tom Cusack. "Peter said Jake used to be a police service dog."

"Honorably retired," said Jackie. "He's not a young dog—about eight, I'd say. Maybe a bit more."

"Well, that's getting on for a Shepherd," Tom said, opening the door of a low-roofed building to a chorus of barks and whines that almost drowned out his voice. "Even one who's lucky enough not to have the hip or spine problems that are common to the breed is probably starting to feel his age a bit by eight."

"Well, I think he might have slowed down just a bit the last two years," Jackie admitted.

"That's natural," said Tom, "but it doesn't mean he's finished, or even close to it. Old dogs can still learn plenty of new tricks. Take me, for instance."

Jackie laughed. "You're an old dog, huh?"

"Well, I've been pretty set in my ways. I'd never lived anywhere but California, but I found out I could still learn a trick or two. I left everything familiar behind, and came two thousand miles to start something completely new here in Palmer." He indicated his new enterprise with a sweep of his hand.

"Congratulations on your new trick," said Jackie. "It looks great."

It did look great, Jackie thought—well thought out and well taken care of. The kennel cages were clean and dry, with a supply of fresh food and water, and each allowed its occupant access to a larger run outdoors. Nearly every cage was occupied, and the dogs came to the wire in front as they passed, looking for a bit of attention. It was a little like riffling through an encyclopedia of dog breeds at random, with a sturdy Scots terrier next to a sleek Irish setter, followed by a burly Rottweiler.

"These are our boarders," said Tom, stopping to pat the head of a wriggling Dalmatian. "We're the resort where the dogs stay while their owners are living it up in Florida or the Bahamas, or visiting the grandparents in Springfield."

"No snorkeling or poolside bar service," Jackie noted.

"Well, it's a modest sort of resort," Tom allowed with a smile, "but the rates are cheaper, too." They left the dog building and walked out into a parklike area with hurdles and other obstacles set up in and among the sturdy old trees.

"Is this the obedience course Peter told me about?" Jackie inquired.

"It's all sorts of things depending on how we set it up," said Tom Cusack. "We run trials here sometimes, train pups, put dogs through their paces to see what kind of training they've had—lots of different stuff." They crossed the park and headed back toward the main buildings closer to the driveway. "Here's where the cats stay," Tom noted, opening the door to one of the buildings. Inside was a small room with cages where half a dozen cats lounged, and a play area with carpeted jungle gyms and all sorts of cat toys on strings and wires, bobbing this way and that in the breeze from the screened window.

They stepped inside, and Tom opened the doors to the cages and stopped to pet each feline occupant. "You have any cats at home?" he asked Jackie.

"No, Jake's our only boarder," she said, reaching her fingers inside the mesh of a cage door to stroke the head of a huge orange tomcat with a disgruntled look on his face.

"I'm not sure how Jake would take to the competition."

"That depends on the dog," he said. "Some do better than others handling sibling rivalry."

"We had a puppy of Jake's for a while," Jackie remembered, barely suppressing a shudder at the memory of Maury and the stupendous level of mischief of which he was capable. "Luckily, we found someone who wanted him before he destroyed everything we owned."

"Well, a cat's a different proposition from a puppy," said Tom. "Not so destructive, for one thing, though you do have to train them away from certain behaviors. I've found that when you introduce a young kitten to an older dog, the results are usually surprising. The dog tends to assume ownership of the cat."

"And vice versa, of course," Jackie laughed.

"Of course. And they usually become best friends in a pretty short time, as long as the cat's already had some nonthreatening exposure to dogs." He closed the last cage. "It's something to think about—Jake might enjoy some company when you had to be away from the house during the day, and he probably wouldn't see a cat as competition, unlike a puppy."

Outside the doors to the cat room, the rest of the area was set up for bathing and grooming, with stainless steel sinks and grooming tables, and a freshly painted cement floor sloping toward a large floor drain.

Tom opened a door at the far end of the grooming area, and led Jackie into a pleasant, sunny office with a desk under one window and a sofa near the other. He pointed toward the window, at her car and Jake, who was still waiting patiently to be let out. "Why don't you bring Jake in here?" he offered, "and he and I can get acquainted. I think he's waited about long enough out there."

Jackie let herself out the front door and returned with Jake on his lead. She led the way inside the office, with Jake properly at heel, as though he sensed the importance of being on his very best behavior for this occasion.

Tom approached the Shepherd respectfully, waiting for Jake to size him up before reaching out to scratch him between his huge ears. "He's a fine example of the breed, all right," he commented, smiling at Jackie. "Oh, and there's fresh coffee in the pot over there if you're interested."

"Thanks. Would you like some, too?"

"Black. Thanks." He flashed another smile.

Jackie turned her back on him on the pretext of looking at the coffee things, which had been laid out as if he were expecting to invite her to stay for a cup. She hoped he hadn't seen her flush. Tom's smile was appealing—not a calculated sort of thing, but the kind that wins hearts without ever being aware of it. She found herself wondering if there were a Mrs. Cusack in the picture, and was instantly ashamed of herself for speculating. She'd only just met the man, for God's sake.

She poured two mugs of coffee and turned back around. Tom had hunkered down in front of Jake and was ruffling the fur on his neck. Jake sat happily with that expression of his that was almost a smile, his tail brushing the floor in contented motions. "Is this what they call male bonding?" she ventured.

"It's a guy thing," Tom laughed, giving Jake's head a pat and accepting a mug from Jackie. "You've got a great dog here. Jake's a show-quality Shepherd, aside from his age and some wear and tear." His fingers lingered on the knot of scar tissue on Jake's right front leg, where he'd been shot with a .44 magnum while attempting to defend his previous owner's life. He raised an eyebrow, but didn't ask.

"He doesn't seem to be overbred, either—you know, too long in the body or too narrow in the skull." He turned Jake's face to his and looked him in the eyes. "He's sociable, but not overly eager for attention, and he looks quite intelligent, too.''

"Oh, I can vouch for that," Jackie assured him. Jake's intelligence had helped her out of some sticky situations in the past, and she was grateful for it. She'd never dreamed, in her unregrettably bygone days as a bored suburban housewife, how much a police dog can come in handy when you suddenly find yourself an accidental detective, which had been happening to her all too often since she ended her marriage and brought her young son back to Palmer.

Tom took a seat on one end of the sofa, and Jackie used that as her cue to sit down on the other end. It wasn't that long a sofa, and when they turned around to face one another Jackie couldn't help noticing that their knees weren't all that far apart. She mentally rapped her knuckles. She was here about Jake. Better to keep her mind on that.

Jake was still sitting where Tom had left him, looking at the trainer as if for a cue he hadn't yet received. Tom pointed at the floor in front of the couch, and Jake came over and lay down, settling his head on his paws where he could look back and forth between the two of them.

"So tell me about obedience trials," Jackie said by way of getting her mind back on business.

"Well, we have a training program for that," said Tom, "but frankly, I don't think that's what Jake needs."

"You don't? Why not?" Jackie was surprised that Tom Cusack seemed to be turning away business.

"Because he's been there and done that," Tom said, nodding in Jake's direction. "The training he would have received for police service work far exceeds anything he'd encounter in obedience trials. He's probably been trained in some combination of searching, tracking, sniffing out drugs or illicit cash—the stuff police dog work is made of. I'd say he's almost certainly had some pretty thorough protection training."

"Well, he's protected me a few times," Jackie recalled, smiling at her dog. And he had certainly proved his ability at finding things when he sniffed out the secret cache of old money at Winnie Swann's house the day before.

Jake's tail wagged in response to his mistress's attention. His ears perked up, as if for any mention of his name.

"We could sharpen up some of those skills, if you think they'll be needed," said Tom. "If you're planning on getting lost in the Swiss Alps, for instance. Most people don't know it, but there are more German shepherds doing rescue work over there than there are St. Bernards." The dark blue eyes twinkled above the rim of his mug as he took a sip of his coffee.

"Well, that could come in handy, I guess," Jackie allowed. She couldn't seem to stop herself from smiling at Tom, though she did her best to make it look friendly and impersonal. She hoped it was working.

"I'd have to work with him a bit to be sure," said Tom, "but I suspect all Jake needs is a reminder of his training, and some activities that'll let him practice the things he already knows. There are trials for tracking and protection, too, but that would mean some very structured activities, getting involved with clubs, traveling around to trials . . ."

"I'm not sure how practical that would be," said Jackie.

"I'm not sure how much fun it would be for you and Peter compared to just making up some games for Jake that will use the abilities he's developed in a less structured atmosphere. All intelligent dogs love to play, and Shepherds are no exception. Boredom is bad for everybody, dogs and people, too. Working dogs, though, are a special case. They love to work. In short, you might say that a Shepherd needs a job."

"Jake's occupation is pretty much limited to fetching a ball these days." Except for the job he'd done yesterday. And he'd seemed more like his old self ever since finding the money. Maybe Tom Cusack was right, she thought.

"But that hardly seems like enough for him, does it?"

"I don't think he's old enough yet to limit him that much," Tom agreed. "What would you say to trying Jake out with some tracking?"

"How would that work?"

"You could bring Jake and Peter here one day soon and I'd be glad to show you. Or we could meet someplace else, maybe that big old wooded area east of town on the Fairborn Road. Are you familiar with it?"

"Well, it's been a few years since I've been out there. My parents used to take me out there for picnics, I remember. I don't think I'd have too much of a problem finding it again."

"Good." Tom got up and took an appointment calendar off his desk. "Here we go," he said, sitting back down on the sofa. "How about Saturday?"

"Tomorrow?"

"Sure. Why not? If it's okay with you, that is."

"It'd have to be after lunchtime, I guess—Peter goes to karate class at ten."

"At the Kenpo dojo on Sixteenth Street?"

"Yes. How did you know?"

"That's where my daughter goes. Every Saturday at ten."

"Daddy?" A young girl's voice called from just outside the door.

"Perfect timing," laughed Tom. "That's Grania—my daughter. In here, sweetheart."

A lovely girl about Peter's age stepped into the office. She was slender, with light brown hair and startling green eyes. "Hello," she said to Jackie, before leaning down to kiss her father's cheek.

"Grania, this is Jackie Walsh. And this is Grania Cusack, only daughter and light of my life."

"Pleased to meet you." She smiled at Jackie—a lovely and natural smile, devoid of teenaged self-consciousness.

"Are you Peter Walsh's mother?" Grania held out her hand, and Jackie shook it, impressed with the girl's poise and friendliness.

"Yes, I am," she replied, *and you must be the reason my son's so interested in dog training all of a sudden*, she thought to herself. She couldn't help smiling. If Peter was finally starting to show some interest in girls, he had certainly picked a great one to start with.

"Well, I've gotta go," Grania excused herself with a wink for her father that Jackie clearly wasn't meant to see. "Nice meeting you, Ms. Walsh."

"Nice meeting you, too, Grania." As she watched the girl walk out and close the office door behind her, Jackie couldn't help wondering what was going on here. First Peter couldn't wait for her to meet Tom Cusack, now this conspiratorial behavior from Grania, Peter's school and dojo classmate. It was beginning to look like she was being set up. The question was, she thought, looking out of the corner of her eye at the handsome dog trainer, did she really mind?

CHAPTER 11

After leaving the kennels, a bit later than she had intended on account of how much fun she had had talking to Tom Cusack, Jackie gave her mother a call and arranged to meet at Winnie's house as soon as she could be on that side of town. Frances had already located Barney Dorfmeier through his granddaughter's telephone listing. When she'd called the house Mrs. Batcheler said he was out of town until tomorrow, visiting great-grandchildren in Cleveland. Jackie hoped she'd be so peripatetic when she was on the shady side of ninety. She had no doubt her mother would.

Frances was eager to make another visit to Winnie's house, and Jackie had to smile at the air of conspiracy her mother managed to inject into it when they'd spoken over the phone. She'd berated Jackie for taking so long at the kennels, and she was already waiting impatiently when Jackie pulled up in front of the old house on Willow Street.

This time Jake entered the Swanns' house with an air of anticipation and eagerness. Finding the money in the living room wall where Franklin Swann had hidden it behind the framed print seemed to have energized him. Maybe it was like Tom Cusack had said—a German Shepherd needs a job. Finding things was one of the jobs Jake had been trained to do well, and much like a person, he seemed to take pride in a job well done. He trotted over to the spot where all the excitement had taken place and sat there wagging his tail as if wondering how they might top that experience today.

"You're a very good, very smart dog, Jake," Jackie assured him, and he sat there, proud and alert, and looked as if the praise were only his due, after all. Well, perhaps it was, Jackie thought—who'd know better than Jake?

Jackie and Frances had driven in another nail above the damaged part of the wall and replaced the print over the gaping hole before they had swept up the dust and pieces of plaster so that the house would look undisturbed to anyone looking in from the outside. Now Frances went to the window to make sure no one was close enough to see inside while they disturbed the scene one more time. "Wait just a minute, Jackie," she warned. "There's a man walking by."

"The next-door neighbor?"

"I don't know what the neighbor looks like, and I can't see this one's face, but he's a skinny little fella about five-foot-three, wearing black gloves."

"Oh, I think he lives around here somewhere—I saw him outside the other day. Is he gone yet?"

"Yep. Just turned the corner. Go ahead, take the picture down. I'll keep lookout."

It was a good thing someone was enjoying this, Jackie thought. Frances was having more fun with this little adventure of theirs than she'd probably had in years. Even those Thursday night poker games of old had nothing like this to offer—murder, robbery, ill-gotten gains—all the things that made life worth living.

Jake watched Jackie's every move as she lifted the heavy frame and set it down on the sofa. Reaching inside the hole, she withdrew a loose twenty-dollar bill and put it inside a white paper envelope she had brought from her office for the purpose. Then she replaced the frame and straightened it carefully before putting the envelope into her handbag. "I guess we should be going now," she told her mother.

"Now just a minute, Jacqueline," Frances began in a tone of voice that Jackie recognized from long experience as the beginning of more trouble. "Winnie told us that Franklin was always fixing things all over the house—walls, floors, and the like. He never stopped, to hear her tell it. What do you want to bet that means he had other hiding places as well?"

"Oh come on, Mother," said Jackie, barely bothering to hide her impatience. "Why can't you be satisfied with just *one* hoard of illicit cash?"

"Where's your sense of adventure, child?" her mother wanted to know. "I thought *you* were the detective in the family. Shouldn't we know what else might be hidden around here? After all, you've got the expert in hidden money right there on the end of that leash." She pointed to Jake, who wagged his tail some more and gave his mistress an eager look. Frances's best ally, it seemed, was Jackie's own dog.

Jackie knew a losing battle when she saw one. "Okay, Mother," she sighed. "My money-sniffing dog is at your disposal. Where would you like to start?"

"Let's just take a stroll around the house and see what we can see," Frances suggested. "Or smell, rather. Bring the expert with you." She led the way into the kitchen, and Jackie and Jake followed dutifully.

Jake sniffed his way around the kitchen and bedrooms, pausing here and there to take interest in a particular scent, but without once showing the kind of excitement that had marked his discovery of the hidden money the day before. After fifteen minutes or so of this, Jackie was prepared to call it quits, but Frances Costello would have none of it.

"We haven't checked out the bathroom," she pointed out.

Jackie knew her mother would never be satisfied that

there was no more evidence to be found until she had let Jake get a whiff of every square inch of the little house. She led Jake to the bathroom doorway. "I don't think there's room in there for all three of us," she said. She unclipped Jake's lead and let him have the bathroom to himself while she and her mother waited outside in the narrow hallway, watching.

Jake stuck his nose into every corner of the little bathroom without showing any particular excitement, and Jackie, nearly as relieved as Frances was disappointed, snapped her fingers for him to return to her side. He trotted halfway across the floor, then stopped and began scratching at one of the floor tiles near the door. He whined once, then looked up at his mistress and began to bark.

"I told you so," said Frances with unmistakable smugness.

"Oh, no, not again!" Jackie moaned. "Jake, stop scratching that floor!" She knew, even as she said it, that it was a useless command, but she figured she had to try anyway.

Jake stopped and sat back on his haunches, but he continued to whine, cocking his head and looking at Jackie as though she weren't too bright.

"I'll go and find a knife, and then we can loosen that floor tile," said Frances, disappearing into the kitchen.

Jackie returned Jake's stare. "You're still a very good dog," she told him, "but you're sure making a lot of trouble for everyone."

"It was Franklin who made the trouble," said Frances, back from the kitchen. She handed Jackie a sturdy butter knife. "Now it's our job to fix everything up again for poor Winnie. Get to it, girl."

"Come on out of there, Jake," Jackie said, and Jake walked away from the spot he'd been guarding, seeming relieved that someone was finally going to do something about his latest discovery.

Jackie turned on the bathroom light and got down on her knees by the place Jake had been scratching—the center floor tile nearest the doorway. She slipped the blade of the knife in between that tile and the one next to it, and pried carefully upward. "I hope I don't break this," she muttered. "It's bound to be glued down pretty tight."

To her surprise, the tile lifted quite easily. When she lifted it up and examined it, she could see that the adhesive on its back side was a different kind from what she had used to tile her bathroom and kitchen in the townhouse—more like rubber cement—though the tiles on all sides of it seemed to be anchored tightly in the usual way.

She looked carefully at the floor underneath the loose tile. At first nothing seemed out of the ordinary—just plywood floor under the old two-toned green asphalt tiles, but assuming that the loosely glued tile had to be significant in some way, she looked more carefully.

Her closer inspection showed that the floorboards had been sawn just at the edges of the tile, and there were two depressions in the wood, about an inch apart. They looked like random chips in the wood at first glance, but they were just the right size to put her fingers into.

She grasped it and lifted. The loose square of plywood came clear, revealing a small open area like a little box. Inside that was a carefully wrapped package, covered in brown paper, tied with string, and finished off with a neat bow. Jackie took a deep breath and lifted it out.

"What is it, Jackie? What is it?" Frances was practically dancing in the doorway in her eagerness to know what Jackie had found. "Bring it over here where I can get a better look at it."

"It's not more money," Jackie said, getting to her feet and brushing off the knees of her jeans. "The package is too small for that. Sorry." She held up the package, which measured perhaps two inches by five, and was less than an inch thick. "I wonder if we should unwrap it?"

Frances looked at her daughter in disbelief. "Of course we should unwrap it, foolish child." She shook her head at Jackie's obtuseness. "How else will we ever find out what's inside?"

"Good point," Jackie conceded. She carried the package into the living room, and Frances followed eagerly, with Jake bringing up the rear. She stood in the light from the living room windows and untied the string, then unwrapped the layer of brown wrapping paper to reveal a small white gift box.

"Maybe it's jewelry," Frances speculated. "The box is about the right size for a bracelet. Diamonds, perhaps? Emeralds? I've always preferred emeralds, personally."

Jackie felt a pang of impatience at her mother's fantasizing. "Franklin was a bank robber, Mother—not a jewel thief." She couldn't deny, though, a growing feeling of curiosity as she broke a seal of cellophane tape around the edge of the box, lifted the lid, and encountered a layer of white cotton wool. Maybe Frances wasn't so far off, after all.

She lifted up the cotton to find a small, roughly cylindrical item, nearly black in color, bent in two places, and twisted, like a piece of old wood. Something about its shape was familiar. She brought it closer to the light and looked again.

"What's that on the end of it?" said Frances, pointing. It looks almost like a . . ." she gasped, her face going stark white.

Jackie echoed her a moment later. "A fingernail! Oh, my God . . ." she dropped the package and the mummified finger fell out of its box and rolled across the floor, with Jake in hot pursuit, claws scrabbling and feet slipping on the hard surface of the floor.

"Jake, no!" Jackie screamed, launching herself at her dog and the awful item he was about to put in his mouth. She skidded stomach down on the floor, burning the skin from her forearms on the polished wood, her hand covering the finger an instant before Jake's teeth would have closed on it.

She wavered between relief, pain, and horror—she was holding a human finger! It didn't feel much like a finger, she tried to tell herself as she sat up, still clutching it. Jake panted happily, ready for round two of the chase-the-finger game.

Jackie stood up carefully, holding her arm out as far as possible from her body. Frances had retrieved the box, which had fallen to the floor in the excitement, and Jackie shuddered as she dropped the finger back inside, closed the lid, then checked to see if she was going to faint. She wasn't, as it turned out, but her arms stung something awful.

There was a loud rattle in the front door lock, then the door flew open, banging against the wall, and a man and woman somewhere in their sixties stood in the doorway, staring at Jackie and Frances. "What the hell are you doing in my house?" shouted the man.

CHAPTER 12

Jackie slipped the box containing the dried finger into her shirt pocket, and tried not to wince as her sleeves rubbed against her raw forearms. Blood was beginning to seep through the cloth. "Your house?" she said to the man, astonished. "Excuse me, but who are you?"

"I'm Dalton Swann," said the man, who was thin and pale, and not at all as handsome as his father had been, with dyed black hair slicked back from a high forehead over narrow eyes and thin lips. The surface resemblance was there, but a person's face was what they made of it by Dalton Swann's age, and he had made something rather repellent of his.

"And this is my sister, Claire Brumbaugh." He indicated the short, plump woman beside him, whose face—complete with shoe-button eyes, jutting jaw, and a severely upturned nose—wouldn't have been very out of place on an English Bulldog. Claire must take after her mother, Jackie thought, or perhaps a family pet.

"We're here from Columbus to check on my property. I inherited this house from my late father upon his death last month."

"Oh, you must be Franklin's children!" exclaimed Frances, stating the obvious with rare talent.

The ones Winnie said she'd have drowned, Jackie thought, and noting the sour looks on their disagreeable faces, she had to admit a certain amount of sympathy for that idea. "We're friends of Winnie's," Jackie told them. "I'm Jackie Walsh and this is my mother, Frances Costello." She held out a hand.

"Friends of Winnie's," said Dalton Swann, his lip curling in noticeable distaste. "How nice." He took Jackie's hand in a moist, flaccid grip. She made herself resist checking it for mildew when she got it back a second later.

"*Friends of Winnie's, Claire*," Dalton shouted at his sister. "Claire's hard of hearing," he explained in a voice she was clearly not meant to hear, "but she refuses to admit it, so she won't get a hearing aid. *Winnie*!" he repeated at the top of his lungs when she didn't seem to hear him the first time.

"Old homewrecker," Claire muttered, her lower lip quivering, and her little piggy eyes brimming with deep and malevolent emotion. Evidently the utter lack of affection between Winnie and her husband's children was mutual.

"Father left me the house in his will," Dalton explained. "I know he didn't want to," he added, lips drawn back primly, "but it was a condition of his inheriting it from his father that it had to be left to the eldest son. He consulted lawyers about it, but to no avail. Grandfather's contract was watertight." He smiled a thin, straight smile of satisfaction, presumably at having won the grand prize in the last game of Franklin Swann's life.

If Jackie had been reserving judgment on whether or not she disliked Dalton Swann intensely, that smile would have weighted the scales.

"But what do you expect Winnie to do?" Frances asked indignantly. Jackie could see her mother's hackles rising at the thought of her friend left without a roof over her head. "Without this house, she'll be left with no means of support!"

"I'm sure Father provided for his *wife*," said Dalton, making the word seem unpalatable in the extreme, and looking at Frances for the first time. "And if he didn't, well, it's really no concern of ours, is it?" He turned back to Jackie. "So might we ask what brings you to the house, Mrs. Walsh?"

"It's *Ms.* Walsh, and we were just looking for something Winnie needed at the convalescent home." Not bad for off the top of her head, she thought, pausing to congratulate herself. Not even that far from the absolute truth, if it came to that. She had a sudden, very frightening thought, and stopped herself from looking behind her at the cockatoo print that covered a gaping hole in the wall full of stolen money. "Will you and your sister be staying at the house?"

Dalton looked around the little living room with an expression of repugnance that seemed somehow natural on his pale, pinched face. "We have rooms at the Palmer Inn," he said. "Our only interest in the house is to see that it's prepared for sale as quickly as humanly possible."

"Then perhaps you wouldn't mind if we stayed and gathered up Winnie's belongings as a favor to her." Jackie flashed him a wide smile.

"I'm sure that would be all right," Dalton said, a slight flush rising to color his pallid cheeks. "*Can they stay and pack up Winnie's belongings?*" he yelled at Claire.

"If they don't, I'll burn 'em," she replied. She set her formidable jaw and glared at Jackie. She glanced around the room, tiny eyes flicking from one object to another. When she noticed Jake, she yelped and leapt behind her brother. "They've got a dog in here!" she screamed.

Jake began to bark. It wasn't like him to show alarm, so Jackie decided he was probably just expressing his dislike for the two of them. Claire screamed again and buried her face in Dalton's back.

Dalton put a protective arm up to ward off the perceived threat of Jake. "Claire's frightened of dogs," he explained, patting his sister's meaty arm. "You'd best take the beast outside."

"Mother?" Jackie appealed to Frances. She didn't want Dalton and Claire to start inspecting the house unless she was there to lead them away from the cockatoo print.

"Come on, beast," said Frances, taking up Jake's lead and walking him out the front door. Jake stopped in the doorway and looked back over his shoulder at Claire, who was still wailing into the back of her brother's seersucker sports coat, and clinging to him like a drowning woman in a whirlpool. He turned away and let out something very like a sigh as Frances led him away.

Jackie stood facing Franklin's children, if you could even call people their age children, and they stared at her for several seconds while she tried to think of something intelligent to say, with a wall full of contraband cash behind her and a mummified human finger in her pocket. She quickly rejected politics, religion, sports, sex, and the state of the weather as topics of conversation. "Can I call you a cab?" was the best she was able to do, and on reflection it wasn't all that intelligent, really.

"We rented a car at the airport," said Dalton. "I suppose we should be getting over to the Palmer Inn. Claire needs a nap. *Don't you, Claire? Need a nap*?" He shouted.

"Yeah, it's all crap." Claire replied, looking around at the furnishings.

Dalton shook his head. "There'll be a real estate broker here to look at the house first thing Monday morning. I'd appreciate it if you didn't leave a mess." He took his sister's arm, turned, and walked out the front door just in time to nearly bowl over Frances, who was on her way back in.

"What's your hurry?" Frances muttered to their departing backs.

"Thank God they're gone," said Jackie as soon as she was absolutely certain they were out of earshot. "We've got to plaster over that hole in the wall."

"Not before we take the money out of it," said Frances. "We'll probably never be able to get back in here legitimately, and if we leave that money and those two vultures find it in the house, they'll never in a million years allow Winnie to have a cent of it." Her expression dared Jackie to disagree with her. "The house may be theirs, but the money is Winnie's."

"Yeah, for what it's worth, I agree with you," said Jackie. "Of course it might not be worth anything, but that's what we have to find out. Do you suppose there are any supplies for plastering walls in this house?"

Frances snorted. "If Franklin had anything to say about it, I'm sure there are. Let's get busy looking for them."

Frances searched the cabinets for plaster and tools while Jackie pulled bundles of money out of the wall and put them in a paper bag from one of the kitchen drawers. At the very rear of the hole she found another neat packet, this one wrapped in opaque plastic, like a piece of a garbage sack. She stuck it in the bag with everything else, without disturbing the wrapping. She supposed she could always unwrap it later if she felt like she needed another surprise.

CHAPTER 13

The wall repaired, Jackie and Frances set to work packing up the few belongings in the little house. Franklin and Winnie had lived simply and without a lot of pointless possessions. "Franklin was probably traveling light in case he ever found the FBI on his trail," Frances speculated. "With this little stuff they'd be able to pack up and leave in no time."

"What are we going to do about the furniture?" Jackie asked her mother, ignoring her latest fantasy of elderly fugitives from justice. "By rights, it's Winnie's, and Dalton and Claire certainly aren't interested in fighting her for it, but she can't afford to store it, and neither of us has room for it where we live."

"Well, I think between the two of us we should be able to come up with a month's rental on a storage space," said Frances. "That'll give us time to figure it. Maybe she'll want us to sell it."

Jackie looked around her at the furniture and accessories. "You know," she said, "this is going to take us the rest of the day."

"Right as usual, darling daughter," Frances agreed. "So what do you say we quit talking about it and get to work?"

• • •

When Jackie arrived home, exhausted and sore, she found Peter microwaving a brick of frozen vegetarian chili. The smell was wonderful. She hadn't realized how much of an appetite she had worked up, packing and hauling furniture out to a rented van.

"I hope there's enough for me," she said.

"Plenty," Peter assured her. "Where've you been all day?"

She ignored the parental tone—she supposed she had it coming, in a way. She took a brick of cheddar cheese from the refrigerator, and a cheese grater from a drawer. "Let me give you a hand with dinner, chef."

Jackie had to admit that she hadn't spent nearly enough time at home the past few days, but then when she did manage to be home, Peter was usually wrapped up in something else, anyway. Does it count as quality time if the other person is reading a comic book and wearing headphones, she wondered?

"I've been off on a wild goose chase of your grand-mother's," she told him with a sigh of weariness that hadn't been supposed to come out. "It was supposed to be a quick errand, but one thing led to another, and it turned into an all-day hassle."

"Sounds like Grandma, all right," Peter agreed.

Jackie winced for the hundredth time today as her shirt-sleeves rubbed against her raw forearms. Abandoning the cheese for the moment, she rolled up the sleeves carefully and ran cold water over her arms from the kitchen faucet. They stung something fierce.

"How did you do that to yourself, Mom?" her son wanted to know.

"It wasn't easy," she assured him. "Would you go get me some disinfectant and bandages from the bathroom, please?"

Peter returned a few minutes later with all the household first aid supplies, which he set down in a pile on the countertop. It was overkill, but on the other hand, what she needed was bound to be in there somewhere.

"So did you go by and talk to Mr. Cusack?" Peter asked in an elaborately casual tone. Jackie silently congratulated her son on his sharpened interpersonal skills as she sprayed cool anaesthetic liquid onto her skinned arms.

"Yes, I did," she informed him, and was gratified to see his expression change from indifference to delight. "I got a tour of the kennels, and we talked for quite a while. He seems like a very nice man, and he gets along famously with Jake." She liberated several gauze pads from their packages and laid them over the raw skin of one arm.

Peter smiled as he cut lengths of adhesive tape. "I knew you'd like him," he said.

Jackie was about to berate Peter for the embarrassing way he had told Tom Cusack to recognize her. Then she had a better idea for getting to him. "I met his daughter, too," she said casually.

Jackie couldn't remember the last time she'd seen her son blush. She wouldn't forget this time so easily, though— from the collar of his T-shirt all the way up to his scalp, his fair redhead's skin turned a deep shade of pink. He turned away, flustered.

"Help me do the other arm," Jackie said, struggling to keep a straight face. "Then you can get us something to eat with."

"Oh, yeah." Peter finished the gauze and tape, then rummaged for spoons and bowls, and walked them over to the table.

"Tom says Grania's a student in your dojo."

"Uh, yeah. She started there about three months ago, right after they moved to town. She'd studied in San Francisco, though, at a kenpo dojo in the city. That's where they come from."

Jackie's mind went back to her visit to the kennels as she grated the cheese to go on top of the chili. After Grania had visited briefly, then excused herself to do homework, Jackie and Tom had continued their conversation on subjects other than the care and training of German shepherds. Tom had told her that he'd been divorced for the past three years from Grania's mother. He hadn't gone into any personal details, of course, but she could tell from the way he talked about it that his experience with marriage had been at least as unhappy as hers, if not more so.

She could also tell he was interested in her, and the fact that his interest didn't make her in the least uncomfortable was a good sign, she figured. A lot of men found Jackie attractive, but few could attract her interest in turn, and fewer still could hold it for any length of time. It would be interesting to see if Tom Cusack might turn out to be an exception.

"Tom says he thinks Jake needs something besides plain old obedience work," Jackie told Peter, setting the bowl of cheese in the center of the table. "After all, Jake was on the police force for a few years, and Tom says he doesn't need training so much as a reminder of what he already knows. He suggested the four of us ought to get together and run Jake through his paces a bit."

Peter brightened immediately. "When?"

"Saturday—tomorrow. He's got a puppy class until two, then we're meeting them at that big picnic area on Fairborn Road right after that."

"That's great," said Peter with undisguised enthusiasm.

"I thought maybe you'd think so," said Jackie. She didn't mention it to Peter, but she had to admit she thought it might be pretty great, too.

The phone rang just as the microwave beeper went off. Jackie picked up the phone and motioned Peter to get the chili. Cosmo Gordon was on the other end of the line.

"Jackie? How're you doing?"

"Just fine, Cosmo, but I think this may be the first time you've ever called me just to find out." She had her suspicions about what had inspired this friendly call only one day after she had contacted Michael McGowan with her 'hypothetical' problem of stolen money. Cosmo and Michael had been best friends since Michael had first come to Palmer, and they still spoke on the phone frequently, even though Michael was two thousand miles away.

"Well, I've been out of touch with just about everyone since the divorce," said Cosmo, a note of sadness creeping into his voice. "It's taken me a while to get back on my feet socially. You know how that goes, I'm sure."

"I do indeed." Jackie was no stranger to the awkwardness that arises when a couple splits up. Most of the people she'd mistakenly called friends when she was married had remained loyal to Cooper after her marriage to him broke up, and she had found herself suddenly and unpleasantly alone, except for Peter.

Cosmo had probably suffered similarly when he and his wife Nancy divorced recently, and his children were grown and gone now. His job as Palmer's Medical Examiner might keep him too busy to think about his loneliness for long stretches at a time, but eventually it was bound to catch up with him, as it had with her. "I'm glad you called, anyway," she said, "and I'm fine, actually. Peter's fine, too. Jake's especially fine. Now what's really on your mind, Cosmo?"

"Well, I talked to Michael today," Cosmo began.

"Aha."

Cosmo laughed. "It's hard to put one over on you, Jackie."

"Then stop trying. Michael told you he was worried about me after we talked yesterday, didn't he? I'll bet he told you he thought I might be mixed up in something, didn't he?"

"Well, are you?"

"I don't know if 'mixed up' is how I'd put it."

"How would you put it, then?"

"I'd say there've been some interesting happenings lately. I'd be happy to talk to you about it if we could keep it unofficial. Do you have any free time this evening?"

"I would have, but I promised to show up at Dwight Hockersmith's do tonight. I'm not sure why."

"Free food?" Jackie suggested.

"That might have been the reason. It's a good enough one, anyhow," said Cosmo. "Maybe I just needed to get out and mingle with other people for a change. I'm too used to being home with someone, watching T.V."

"Old dogs, new tricks?" Jackie inquired.

Cosmo laughed. "You might say that."

"Well, Mom and I will be there, too, and we're not quite sure why, either. Olin Oliver's going to owe me a whole passel of favors after this election campaign, that's for sure. So let's meet up there tonight. We can talk. Unofficially."

"Unofficially," Cosmo cautioned, "as long as you're not breaking any laws."

Jackie stared at the awful contents of the little gift box she'd found under the floorboards of Winnie Swann's bathroom and wondered if possession of a mummified human finger was against the law. It was certain she wasn't going to drag it along to Dwight Hockersmith's party, though she supposed it would make one hell of an icebreaker for those awkward moments when no one has anything of interest to say. At a time like that, dragging out a little souvenir like this one would certainly liven things up, but aside from a moment of imaginary amusement, she wasn't tempted.

If only she had a picture of it. "Peter!" she called from the doorway of her room to the other end of the upstairs hall that divided the two bedrooms of the townhouse.

"Yeah, Mom?" Peter's voice came back through the door of his room, mixed with the sounds of Black '47 singing "James Connoly."

"Do you still have that Polaroid camera your dad gave you for Christmas?"

"It's in my closet somewhere."

Jackie shuddered. Saying something was in Peter's closet was tantamount to saying it was somewhere in the jungles of Central America. Stanley couldn't have found Livingstone in Peter's closet. "Could you look for it, please?" she begged. "I really need it before I leave for that party tonight."

Jackie couldn't hear the obligatory sigh, but she heard Peter's chair being pushed back from his desk, and the sliding of the closet door, and a quarter-ton of junk falling out onto the floor.

"You need it real bad?"

"Real bad. And I'll owe you a tremendous favor."

"Okay. I'll find it."

"Thanks, babe." An instant picture of the dried-up finger ought to suffice for showing to Cosmo, though she wasn't sure how much he'd be able to tell her that she didn't already know. She closed the little box and put it on her dresser. After a moment's reflection, she covered it with a magazine. Peter would think this grisly little item was just tremendously cool, but Jackie thought it better he didn't know about it just yet—she couldn't imagine explaining this entire mess to him in the time she had left to get ready for Dwight Hockersmith's party.

CHAPTER 14

"So are you enjoying our little get-together?"

Jackie didn't need to turn around to identify Angela Hockersmith at her back, but turn around she did, and with a smile that she hoped looked considerably more sincere than it felt, not that she thought Angela would be an expert on sincerity. "I'm having a great time, thank you, Angela," she said.

Angela was decked out in a shiny teal-blue cocktail dress and dyed-to-match pumps. Her hair was a flawless golden helmet fresh from the stylist's fingers—a triumph of hairspray over gravity. "You look great in that outfit, by the way," Jackie remarked. As long as she was being insincere, she figured, she might as well go for an achievement badge.

"Oh, this old thing," Angela demurred with a practiced flutter of eyelashes. "Now I really like what you're wearing."

Jackie had found her one black rayon dress fallen off the hanger and crumpled up on her closet floor. It had long sleeves, which would cover up the bandages on her arms. She'd thrown it into the clothes dryer with a wet dishtowel to take out the wrinkles, and topped the outfit off with black flats and an emerald green shawl that had been doing duty on top of her dresser. She didn't for a moment think that

Angela really found it attractive, but she knew she looked pretty great. Down and dirty fashion worked every time. "Thanks."

Before she could dredge up something clever to say next, Angela filled in the gap herself. "Didn't I see you and your mother at Forest View Wednesday?"

"We were there, but I don't recall seeing you," Jackie replied cautiously.

"Well, I was there visiting Dwight's mother, who's recovering from surgery, and I just caught a glimpse of you wheeling an old lady out the back door," said Angela. "A relative?"

"A friend," said Jackie. "Winnie Swann."

"Ah, I see. No one I know, I'm afraid," Angela added.

"Dwight told me his father's in his nineties," said Jackie. "And Dwight must be around thirty-five, I would guess."

"Thirty-seven," said Angela. "But he's got such a young face, doesn't he?"

"That must be it," Jackie allowed. "I hope I'm not being rude, but I'm assuming his mother must be much younger than his father, or she had him awfully late in life."

"Dwight is from Dad's second marriage," said Angela. "Loretta—Mrs. Hockersmith, my mother-in-law—is only in her sixties. The first Mrs. Hockersmith died quite a few years back. I never knew her."

Jackie looked around the room for Cosmo. That snapshot was burning a hole in her pocketbook, and she was anxious to know what, if anything, he might make of it.

"Dwight tells me you're a detective," said Angela. "That must be so exciting!"

"Not really," Jackie said.

"Not really exciting?"

"I'm not really a detective."

"But Dwight said that Olin Oliver said that . . ."

"Olin was exaggerating just a bit," said Jackie. Kicking Olin in the shins still seemed like a pretty good idea. "I've been involved on the fringes of a few criminal cases the last couple of years, but nothing official, really."

"Well, official or not, I think it's just fascinating," Angela gushed. "You'll really have to tell me all about it sometime."

Not if I can help it, Jackie thought. "You haven't seen Cosmo Gordon here tonight, have you?" she asked.

"I think he just came in," said Angela, looking around. "Yes, there he is, talking to Dwight over by the punch bowl. Have you sampled our fresh strawberry punch? It's from an old Hockersmith family recipe. The pink bowl has champagne, and the clear bowl is alcohol-free. It's been awfully nice talking to you, Jackie." She patted Jackie on the arm and moved off to charm some other poor guest.

Jackie entertained a moment of curiosity about Angela's sudden friendliness after their less-than-amiable encounter Tuesday night, but she had more important things on her mind to give it too much thought. Angela probably just wanted to ensure Jackie's vote for her husband. Jackie looked across the room at Dwight and wished there were a third candidate. Oh, well—maybe Olin Oliver was right, and Dwight Hockersmith could really do Palmer, Ohio some good. Who was she to say he couldn't?

Dwight, Olin, and Cosmo were talking, laughing, and back-slapping like three political cronies ought to, but they all turned to greet her as she walked toward them. "Here's the young woman I've been waiting to see tonight," said Cosmo, putting an arm around Jackie's shoulders and giving her an affectionate squeeze.

"I'll give you exactly all evening to stop calling me a young woman, Cosmo," said Jackie, smiling at her old friend.

"So, Jackie, can we count on you for some volunteer work down at election headquarters between now and election time?'' Olin Oliver inquired with his best campaign manager smile.

Jackie shot him a look that said ''Don't push your luck,'' and hoped he got the message. What she actually said was ''I'm pretty booked between now and November, Olin, but I'll let you know if I find any spare time in my schedule.''

''Fine, fine,'' said Olin, nodding slowly and steadily like one of those flocked plastic boxer dogs in the back window of a car. ''Just fine.'' The nodding slowed and finally came to a stop. Jackie exhaled with relief. Fascinated by the motion, she hadn't been able to take her eyes off Olin's bobbing head. She blinked and looked over at Dwight.

''How's the campaign coming so far?'' she asked politely.

''So far, so good,'' beamed Dwight, and Jackie wondered if he had a cliché at the ready for every occasion. If he really wanted a career in politics, such a facility would certainly come in handy, she thought.

''Well, you keep up the good fight, Dwight,'' said Cosmo. ''Maybe you can make a real difference in this city. God knows we need one. Jackie, what do you say we have a look at the food Dwight and Angela have laid out for us?'' They turned away toward the long buffet table, where Frances was already loading up on the brie. They picked up plates and flatware and joined the line of people heading purposefully for the evening's featured free meal.

''Now maybe you'd like to tell me what all the mystery's about,'' Cosmo suggested as they stepped up to the table, crowded with food.

''Not while we're eating,'' Jackie told him as she came abreast of the mozzarella fingers. ''But stick around, okay?''

After she'd finished off a plate of Dwight and Angela's free food, Jackie was ready to find a quiet corner somewhere and talk to Cosmo about dismembered digits, but no sooner had they found a likely spot, and Jackie opened her handbag and drawn out the photo, than Dwight and Angela were upon them, smiling, accompanied by a very old man in a natty black pinstripe suit.

Jackie quickly stuffed the snapshot back into her bag and closed the catch.

"Jackie Walsh, I'd like you to meet my father, Judge Henry Hockersmith," said Dwight.

If this was Dwight's ninety-two-year-old father, he was holding up amazingly well, thought Jackie to herself. He was well on the short side of average, several inches shorter than Jackie, even in her bare feet, she guessed. He still had a very nearly full head of white hair, and a posture that suggested a much younger man, though he carried a thick walking stick in the crook of his arm. Its heavy brass top was fashioned in the shape of an eagle's head.

He really didn't look a day over eighty, she thought, and he looked slightly familiar, too, but she had grown up in Palmer, and it was likely she'd seen the Judge's picture somewhere, perhaps when he was still on the bench. She held out her hand, but old Judge Hockersmith only stared at it as though it were a snake that might bite him.

"I never shake hands," he told her finally, looking up to meet her eyes. "It spreads germs." Both hands were firmly buried in the side pockets of his suit as if to protect them from any such unsanitary assault.

Jackie withdrew her hand. "I'm sure it does," she agreed. "Nasty habit, really."

Dwight introduced his father to Cosmo, who had the good sense to learn from Jackie's mistake and not offer his hand for the Judge's disapproval. He settled on a sort of mock salute. Judge Hockersmith nodded curtly. "I know you by reputation, Gordon," he said, and although the look on Cosmo's face made it clear he'd like a bit of illumination on that subject, he was clearly not brave enough to ask Judge Hockersmith just what it was he had heard.

"Angela said she saw you with Winnie Swann," said

Dwight, rushing in to fill the awkward space his father had created.

Angela glared at him with a look that promised an unpleasant future revenge, but Dwight seemed not to notice. "Father went to college with Franklin Swann many years ago."

"Class of '27," said Judge Hockersmith. "Rodgers University."

"Jackie teaches film at Rodgers," Dwight told his father.

"Photography?" the Judge inquired, raising his wispy white eyebrows.

"Movies," Jackie supplied.

The old judge frowned. "Why on God's earth would anyone go to university to study movies?"

"That's an excellent question, Judge Hockersmith," Jackie replied. "I've often wondered the same thing. But as long as they're paying me to teach something I love, I don't want to let on to the administration that the entire department might be totally unnecessary."

Judge Hockersmith frowned into the silence that followed. "Did you know Franklin Swann well?" Jackie asked, hoping to bring the conversation around to a subject that would remove the immutable scowl from the Judge's face.

"Hardly knew him at all in school," said the Judge. "And I don't think I've even seen him in nearly fifty years."

"Are you sure, Dad? I thought you and he were roo . . ."

"Dad's tired, dear," said Angela, patting her husband's shoulder affectionately. "I'm going to help him to bed. You just keep mingling and entertaining our guests, hmmm? I'll be back in a bit." She pointed at a knot of newspaper and television reporters gathered near the pink punchbowl. "Why don't you make sure the media is entertained?"

Dwight brightened. "Good idea, dear." He turned back to Jackie and Cosmo. "I'll just leave you two to talk, and perhaps I'll catch you later," he said before crossing the room to chat up the reporters. Jackie saw Marcella Jacobs among them, and wondered how the uncovering of dirt was coming along. It seemed best not to ask, and Marcella would be busy trying to get something quotable the rest of the evening, anyway.

Jackie shook her head as Dwight walked away. "He looks good on television," she admitted grudgingly.

"Well, maybe that's all it takes," said Cosmo. "He can't be any worse at the job than Jane."

"I suppose not," said Jackie.

"Now what were you going to show me, before we were so rudely and strangely interrupted?"

"Oh, just this," Jackie said, reaching once more into the side compartment of her handbag and withdrawing the snapshot, which she passed over to Cosmo.

He regarded it for quite a few seconds in silence through the bottom halves of his bifocals, then held it up to a nearby lamp for better illumination. "It's a human thumb," he pronounced finally. "Right hand."

"I thought it was a finger," said Jackie, taking the photograph back and examining it herself for a moment. "It's too long to be a thumb, isn't it?"

"The metacarpal bone is still attached to it," Cosmo told her, pointing to the appropriate spot on the picture. "It appears to have been severed from the hand near its base, where it joins the palmar surface."

"Okay. Now look how black and twisted up it is."

"Mummified," said Cosmo. "Dried out."

"Would someone have to do something special to it to make it look like that?" Somehow she had a hard time imagining Franklin Swann performing arcane Egyptian funerary rituals on someone's severed thumb, but if she'd learned anything in thirty-eight years, it was that people are stranger than they have any right to be.

"Probably not. If it were kept in a dry place, it'd probably look about like this after a few weeks or months, depending on the weather.''

"Any guesses how old it is?''

"That would depend on how well it was preserved,'' said Cosmo. "It looks like it's held together pretty well, so either it isn't that old, or someone took very good care of it. Most all of the skin's still there, see?''

"I guess. It all looks like so much dried meat to me.''

"That's pretty much what it is,'' Cosmo agreed. "But more to the point, it's unburied human remains, and there are some very strict laws pertaining to human remains, Jackie.''

Cosmo's serious expression told her she was in for a lecture or worse if she admitted having the thumb. On the other hand she felt awful about the prospect of lying to her old friend. She elected to try a middle path.

"It's just a photograph, Cosmo. I hope there aren't any laws pertaining to photographs of human remains that I'm in danger of bending by having this.'' She held up the offending photo with what she hoped was an expression of total innocence.

Cosmo harrumphed. Jackie almost cracked a smile, but thought better of it.

"No, I suppose not,'' Cosmo admitted. "But I can tell you're up to something. If I could figure out what the hell it is, I'd probably be very angry with you.''

This time Jackie refined the innocent look to near-perfection. "Perish the thought,'' she said. "So tell me. If someone's thumb was, let's say, shot off, could they die of the wound?''

"They might die from loss of blood or even shock, I suppose, if they didn't get medical attention,'' Cosmo allowed. "If they got right to a hospital, though, it mightn't be a terribly serious wound—almost certainly not fatal.'' He looked at her with a certain degree of suspicion. "Why do you ask?''

"Well, wouldn't you? I mean look at this picture. Somebody lost this thumb, after all, and it doesn't seem to have been removed surgically. I just wondered if the person might still be alive." She put the snapshot back into her handbag and snapped it shut. "There's one other thing I'm a little curious about," she said.

"Shoot," said Cosmo with weary resignation. "I can see I'm not going to get you to tell me anything you don't want to about this whole crazy mess, whatever it is."

"You've got that right," said Jackie. "If the person who lost this thumb were still alive, would there be any way of proving it belonged to them?"

"Well, the blood could be typed," said Cosmo, looking down at Jackie from under bushy eyebrows arched like question marks. "But you'd need the actual thumb, and all you have is a photograph."

"You're absolutely right," Jackie said, nodding. "Imagine forgetting that. Silly me."

CHAPTER 15

Jackie and Peter were meeting Tom and Grania Cusack at a wooded picnic area a few miles outside Palmer on Saturday afternoon, but when Jackie got up at six on Saturday morning, she still had nearly eight hours before they even had to get in the car and start for their destination. Plenty of time to take care of some unfinished business regarding Winnie Swann and her outdated money.

She showered, then fixed herself some whole-wheat cereal and opened a carton of vanilla yogurt while she went over everything she knew about the case, writing down facts and remarks on little self-stick notes and applying them to the polished wood surface of the dining room table.

"Okay, we've got Winnie at Forest View." The first little piece of paper, with Winnie's name written on it, went onto the table top. "And we've got Franklin in the ground. Franklin's death was officially declared an accident, but Winnie's sure he was murdered." She added two more notes. "By someone named Lefty," she added dramatically, and scribbled yet another note to place on those two.

"Winnie also says Franklin was a bank robber, and sure enough there's some very old money to back up that notion." The money got its own sticky note, as did the mummified thumb, and between them she put a note wondering why Franklin was hiding these items in the first place.

"Let's not forget Lefty, whoever he is, and whether or not he had anything to do with Franklin's accident," Jackie reminded herself. "Franklin was afraid of Lefty, and said he had something on him." She pondered this for a moment. "What? That he was involved in the bank robbery, of course, but then so was Franklin. Did Lefty have something on him? Did he need anything? Or was there some particular reason Franklin needed that extra edge?" She scribbled out these thoughts and arranged them in a sort of order on the table top.

"And what about Barney Dorfmeier? He and Franklin remained friends the rest of their lives, and they were both involved in the robbery." Barney Dorfmeier got his own note in the sprawling arrangement of little yellow squares.

Jackie stared at the growing collection of little yellow notes while she ate her cereal. If she could just get all the facts down, combine and recombine them, something might leap out at her. Perhaps one of those blinding flashes her mother had talked about. Well, it had worked as far as Jake and the money, she thought. Maybe she'd get lucky today as well.

"Okay, back to Franklin," Jackie said when she'd finished her bowl of cereal. "He fell off a ladder while he was climbing down from his roof. What the hell was a ninety-year-old man doing climbing up on his roof, anyway?" Ninety-year-old men were obviously made of better material these days, Jackie thought. If Franklin was doing his own home repairs at that age, he must not have thought of himself as being particularly old and feeble. The dead might outnumber the living by a long shot, but people were also living longer and remaining healthier than ever before, and Franklin Swann seemed to be a pretty good example of that trend.

"So Franklin had an accident with a ladder. But who says a fall from a ladder has to be accidental?" she asked

herself. ''If I wanted to kill someone and make it look like
an accident, I could always watch for them to do something
potentially dangerous, then exploit the situation.'' She
imagined someone—this Lefty person, perhaps—giving the
ladder a little shove and pitching poor old Franklin to the
ground. The fall mightn't have killed him, of course, but it
did. Lucky for Lefty, unlucky for Franklin.

''Then there's the money.'' She tapped the note referring
to the currency Jake had found, then peeled the top off the
carton of yogurt and lifted out a creamy spoonful. ''Franklin was probably selling it off for its value to collectors.
Didn't Winnie say he went off on trips every spring and
fall? Where did she say he went?'' Her mind went back to
the first day she'd met Winnie Swann, and the things they'd
talked about while they strolled around the grounds of Forest View.

''Chicago, or Indianapolis, or Pittsburgh, is what Winnie
said.'' All major cities within a few hours' drive or bus ride
from Palmer, all sure to have a wide selection of dealers in
rare coins and currency among whom Franklin might have
spread the bills carefully, a few at a time. If Franklin had
remained on friendly terms with Barney Dorfmeier all those
years as Winnie had told her, then it was likely that he was
splitting the proceeds with him, and probably with the mys-
terious Lefty as well.

She made a note about the congenial division of the
money with Barney Dorfmeier, and glanced at the dining
room clock. It was still too early to make social calls, but
she had plenty of time later in the morning to go by and
see him. She wondered how forthcoming he was likely to
be about his part in an unsolved bank robbery that had
happened seventy years ago. If he'd guarded this secret for
the majority of his life, how eager would he be to tell her
anything about it now? She hoped she could convince him
that she had no intention of taking anything she knew about
that crime to the police, however guilty she might occa-

sionally feel about that. Besides, she told herself, if she did, her mother would kill her.

"Okay, the money, and later the finger. Thumb, rather. A right thumb. So that's what Franklin had on Lefty. His right thumb. Ha!" She made a note for the thumb and congratulated herself on finally figuring out something that should have been obvious some time back. Well, she'd had a lot on her mind lately.

"Mom?" Peter called down from his room. "Are you talking to yourself?"

"Maybe just a little," Jackie confessed sheepishly. "Did I wake you?"

"Yeah, but I've got to work out before we get ready to go, so don't sweat it."

"Let your weights down easy," she reminded him as she heard the sound of dumbbells being moved around. "These floors are old."

"The money, the thumb, and something else," Jackie continued, a little quieter now. "What was it?" Then she remembered the extra package she'd found in the wall. She put down the yogurt and went into her bedroom, coming back with the neatly wrapped plastic bundle she'd hidden away with the bundles of old money. Unwrapping it with a little chill of anticipation, she discovered half a dozen packets of twenty-dollar bills—honest-to-God, spendable United States twenties.

"Darn," Jackie said to herself. "I was expecting something to top that mummified thumb." She scolded herself mentally for being too much like her mother for her own comfort. And anyhow, she asked herself, how do you top a mummified human thumb? That was a question she wasn't sure she wanted to answer.

The little bands around the outside of each packet of bills said $500. "That's three thousand dollars in real money! Winnie isn't quite broke after all." What a relief. Tomorrow she and Frances would take the money to Winnie at

Forest View, and her bill would be paid for a couple of months. After that, who knew? Well, it was a beginning, anyhow. She finished her yogurt and reached for the phone book. A city the size of Palmer was sure to have a large selection of dealers in rare coins and currency.

Before she could pick up the phone, it rang, startling her. "Jackie, it's your mother," Frances announced, as though her daughter could mistake her for anyone else. "Noreen Smith just called me from Forest View."

"Noreen, Winnie's nurse, you mean?"

"That's her. She says Winnie's house has been burglarized! I'm going over there right now."

"I'll meet you there," Jackie told her. "Peter!" she called as she hurried up the winding iron staircase to her bedroom. "I have to go out for a while. I'll be back as soon as I can."

Peter stuck his head out of his bedroom door as she went past. "You're not going to make us late to meet Mr. Cusack and Grania, are you?"

"Don't worry," she assured him over her shoulder as she reached her room and flung her bathrobe over a chair, "We don't have to leave until nearly two, and I'll be back well before then."

Peter's door closed right after that with no further admonitions or arguments, so Jackie was left to assume that he took her at her word. She went to her closet and pulled out her best pair of jeans and a dark green silk shirt that ought to be just perfect on a day like this one.

She might as well dress for the afternoon now, in case she didn't make it home in time to change before they left. She added a pair of Rockport ankle-high boots and took a light cotton sweater in case the weather changed. Digging through her meager collection of cosmetics, she chose a lip gloss and tossed it into her handbag, just in case she wanted an extra edge in the glamour department sometime today.

She regarded herself in the mirror over her dresser. Okay,

she wasn't twenty-two any more, nor would she want to be even if someone paid her, and there were a few gray streaks in the hair, and a few fine lines around her mouth and eyes that hadn't been there ten years ago, but she was holding up pretty well, she thought. She studied her reflection, decided the finished product was as good as it was going to get, then snatched up her car keys and rushed out the door.

CHAPTER 16

The police were out in force on Willow Street, and a cordon of yellow and black crime scene tape had been thrown up all around Winnie's house—strung around trees and shrubs and the mailbox like bizarre party streamers. It was difficult to recognize this as the same quiet little house she'd visited twice before, owing to the addition of a corps of detectives, uniformed officers, and evidence technicians with cameras and fingerprint equipment walking this way and that.

There was a small crowd of neighbors and passers-by on the scene, murmuring speculations among themselves, and Frances was waiting for her—not patiently, however—at the perimeter, having already failed to gain entrance to the crime scene itself.

"I told them we were friends of Winnie's," Frances told Jackie, obviously wounded by the uncaring attitude of local law enforcement, "but they told me to stay behind the line and not annoy the officers."

"Always good advice, Mother," said Jackie. She looked inside the open door to the house, where even with all the police officers and evidence people confusing the scene it was easy to see that the house had been torn apart. Even from this distance she could see gaping holes in the walls of the living room.

"You've got a lot of nerve coming back here!" said an angry voice behind her.

Jackie turned to see Dalton Swann, sister Claire in tow, walking toward them with a stride so determined it threatened to topple him over frontwards. "Oh, hello, Mr. Swann," she said as politely as she could manage. "What happened here?"

"Someone broke into my house and ripped apart the floors and walls, that's what happened!" Dalton shouted. "And the last people I saw in this house were you two!" He jabbed an accusing finger at each of them in turn. Claire said nothing, but fixed them with a belligerent stare.

"Mr. Swann, you can't possibly think we had anything to do with this . . ."

"What'd she say?" Claire asked her brother.

"I certainly can," Dalton replied, ignoring his sister and shaking his finger in Jackie's face. "I leave my house in perfect condition with you two in it, and the next time I see it, it's been destroyed!" He waved an arm at the destruction in question. Jackie couldn't argue the facts as Dalton had spoken them, but she felt she ought to find fault with his interpretation of how those facts fit together.

"Mr. Swann, just because we're the last people you saw in the house—" she'd refuse to call it his house, even if he put bamboo slivers under her fingernails—"doesn't mean we had anything to do with this crime."

"Doesn't mean you didn't, either," Dalton riposted with more world-class logic. "Where were you late last night when this supposedly happened?"

Jackie bristled. "I don't have to answer that question," she informed him, arms crossed in front of her chest in a gesture meant to convey every bit of the animosity she was feeling right now.

Unable to hear the particulars, Claire turned her head from one to the other, her formidable jaw set in a pose that reminded Jackie of a hostile, attack-trained Pekinese. Looking at Claire, she had a hard time keeping a straight face in spite of the gravity of the immediate problem.

"You were right the first time, Jacqueline," Frances said, glaring at Dalton with an intensity that made Jackie wince. "He can't possibly think." She gave him a frown that would sour milk.

Dalton turned his ire—and his finger—on Frances. "I'll bet Winnie put you up to this!" he said. "It'd be just like her to get back at me for getting the house. The old troublemaker—I'll sue her for everything she's got!"

"That shouldn't take long," Frances commented. "She hasn't got anything, thanks to you."

"What'd she say? What'd she say?" Claire asked, bouncing on her toes in her eagerness to be let in on the conversation.

Dalton was momentarily speechless, but his mouth continued to move convulsively, as if he were doing an impression of a landed fish.

Jackie noticed a familiar form standing in the doorway, and waved to Evan Stillman, a detective in the Palmer Police Department whose acquaintance she had first made soon after she had come back to town, around the same time she had met Michael McGowan. They hadn't exactly been friends, so she hadn't seen much of him since she and Michael had split up, but he was always reasonably friendly when they did meet, and if luck was with her, she could turn that to her advantage. "Hi, Evan!" she called to him.

"Hi, Jackie," Evan called back. "Duck under the tape and come on up. They've already done the walk—just don't step on the grass or they'll be photographing your shoeprints for posterity."

Jackie pulled the tape up and went under it. "Not you, Mother," she said as Frances started to join her on the other side. "I'll only be a minute." She couldn't resist giving Dalton Swann a look of pure triumph as she cleared the tape and let it back down right in front of him.

"Long time no see," said Evan as she joined him on Winnie's front porch. "No one in town get murdered on your beat lately?"

Evan was a bit conservative, Jackie remembered, and he liked things 'by the book,' and while he'd been pleasant enough to her since she started becoming involved in these strange happenings over the last couple of years, Jackie was sure, knowing Evan, that there was a part of him that rebelled deeply at the idea of a citizen—an amateur—investigating cases that were within the official purview of the Palmer Police Department.

She supposed she couldn't blame him, really; he had all the years of training and the experience, and all she had was the bad luck to keep stumbling across murders, and the worse luck to be in a position to help solve them. She was damned if she was going to tell him anything about this one, if indeed Franklin's death was actually anything other than an accident, which was nothing like a sure thing.

"I guess I've been lucky," was her chosen reply, which wasn't exactly the truth, but wasn't exactly a lie, either. That would have to be good enough for now, she supposed.

Evan nodded, as if he might be thinking that her luck was his luck, too. "So what brings you to the scene of a routine burglary, if you don't mind my asking?"

"I don't know if routine's a word I'd use to describe it, Evan," Jackie said, waving her hand at the interior of the little house. From here she could see that every wall in the living room had been reduced to piles of plaster chunks and drifts of powder lying on the floor between the two-by-four studs that made up the walls' frames. Additionally, floorboards had been pried loose from floor joists and left sticking up at odd angles with bent nails protruding from their ends. The evidence technicians picked their way around the mess with care, cursing frequently and expertly. "Are routine burglars usually this thorough?"

Evan didn't dignify Jackie's remark, but crossed his

arms, seeming to wait for a straight answer to his original question.

Jackie sighed. "I'm a friend of Winnie Swann, the owner of the house."

"Now that's interesting," Evan commented. "There's a gentleman over there who claims to own the house." He pointed at Dalton, who was still staring open-mouthed and bug-eyed at Jackie. "That guy in the ugly suit who looks like he just stuck his finger into a light socket."

"He's a technicality," Jackie told him. "Okay, I suppose he does actually own it, but he stole it from an old woman who lived here for fifty years."

Evan looked at Dalton again. "Yeah, he looks capable of that," he said.

"You're an excellent judge of character," Jackie assured him. "So what's up? Anything you can tell me about this?"

"You're assuming I want to tell you anything about it in the first place," said Evan, but he managed a smile as he said it.

"Oh, come on, Evan. After all those glamorous, exciting murder cases you think I'd be caught dead stooping to investigate a routine burglary? Where's the thrill in that? I'd just like to be able to have something to tell Mrs. Swann when I go visit her in the rest home." She gave the last two words as much subtle emphasis as she could muster up, hoping for a bit of sympathy. She got it.

"So far not a print anywhere, and nothing conveniently left behind that would identify our perp," Evan told her with a sigh. "So my guess is he's either a really lucky sonofabitch, or several degrees smarter than the average burglar. What we'd like to be able to figure out is why anybody would burgle an empty house, and what they thought they were going to find in the walls or under the floor. It's not just this room," he said, gesturing inside the open doorway. "It's every damned room in the house. Even the bathroom."

"Kind of sounds like drugs, doesn't it?" Jackie commented.

"Kind of, but who should we suspect? The clueless schmuck in the seersucker suit over there, or the little old lady in the rest home?"

"Hey, don't ask me," Jackie said, shaking her head, "I'm just an amateur."

"Yeah, right."

"How about the neighbors?" Jackie inquired. "Did they see or hear anything?"

"The house on the east side is empty," Evan reported, pointing in that general direction. "It's been up for sale for months. We haven't been able to locate the neighbors on the west side yet."

"Well, thanks," said Jackie. "I know Mrs. Swann will be happy to hear you're on top of it. Give me a call sometime when you're in my neighborhood, and we'll do lunch or something."

"Sure thing," Evan replied. "You take it easy, Jackie."

She gave him a wave, then turned and started down the sidewalk toward Frances and Dalton and Claire and the small knot of curious citizens soaking up the drama of the moment on Willow Street.

"Well, what did he say?" Frances and Dalton asked simultaneously.

"Sorry. Confidential police business," was her reply to Dalton. "Come on, Mom, we've got things to talk about."

"*What did they say*?" Claire screeched.

"Oh, shut up," Dalton grumbled.

CHAPTER 17

"What did you find out?" Frances wanted to know as soon as they were down the sidewalk and out of earshot of Dalton.

"Not a damned thing, but there's no reason for him to know that," Jackie told her mother, gesturing back over her shoulder at Dalton Swann. She didn't even have to look back at him to know there was steam coming out of his ears. Jackie supposed it was juvenile to get such a kick out of his predicament, but she didn't let that stop her from enjoying it anyway.

"Well, what did that young detective say to you, Jacqueline? He must have had some information—you can't have been discussing the Indians' latest losing streak that whole time."

"He says whoever did it left no solid evidence behind, or at least none they've found so far," Jackie reported. "He also said he'd like to know what they could possibly have been looking for."

"I'll bet he would," said Frances with a little smile. "You didn't tell him, did you?"

"Give me some credit, Mother."

"Of course, dear." Frances looked back at Dalton, who was shouting something at Claire. "And imagine that nasty little man having the nerve to think we burgled his father's house.''

''Well, be fair, Mother—we did sort of burgle it, didn't we?''

Frances drew herself up to her full height of five feet and one inch and looked indignant. She was very good at it. ''We most certainly did not,'' she informed her daughter in a tone of voice that brooked no argument. ''All we did was go into the house—with a key and with permission of someone who's practically the owner.''

''Practically,'' said Jackie dryly.

''And remove something that rightfully belonged to someone else,'' Frances concluded.

''Yeah. A bank.''

''A nonexistent bank,'' Frances countered. ''We can't very well travel back in time and return the money, now can we?''

Jackie shook her head. ''I suppose not.'' And if she were going to be one hundred percent honest with herself, she supposed, *she didn't really want to.* The person who would benefit most from that money would be Winnie Swann, and no amount of trying to make herself guilty over it would make her feel any differently. So she wouldn't get an achievement badge with oak leaf clusters in Good Citizenship this time. So what?

An older American sedan cruised sedately down the street from the west and pulled up in front of the house next door. Jackie recognized Ed Woodrow behind the wheel. She looked back at the Swann house, but Evan was inside again, and if· he stepped back out onto the front porch, the hedge between the two houses ought to hide the car from casual observation.

She walked up to the car, Frances following close behind. ''Hi, Mr. Woodrow,'' she said. ''Remember me? Jackie Walsh?''

''Why certainly,'' said Ed Woodrow with a smile as he

stepped out of his car. "You're the one who was here doing Winnie a favor the other day."

"That's right. And this is my mother, Frances Costello. She was here, too, but you two didn't have a chance to meet."

"I'm very pleased to meet you," said Mr. Woodrow, shaking Frances's hand heartily. "Claudia, come on out and meet these nice women. They're friends of Winnie Swann's."

Mrs. Woodrow, a sweet-looking, plumpish woman wearing a little flowered hat, got out of the car on the passenger side, and more introductions were made all around. "Been out for a drive?" Jackie asked.

"An overnight stay at a lovely country inn," said Mrs. Woodrow, favoring her husband with glance of pure romantic affection. "Ed won a contest."

"A contest! Really!" Jackie tried to sound more surprised than she felt. This was getting interesting. "What kind of contest, Mr. Woodrow? Did you have to answer a trivia question or something?"

"Ed's helpless at trivia," Mrs. Woodrow confided. "If it had been anything like that, we'd have been right out of luck. This was just a random phone call kind of thing."

"Yep," Ed confirmed. "Some new radio station in town just called me up one afternoon and told me I'd been awarded a prize. Afterwards I tried to find it on the dial, but I guess it's so new my old Packard Bell won't bring it in!" He laughed at his own little joke, and Jackie and Frances laughed with him. Mrs. Woodrow smiled indulgently.

"Then the other day the envelope arrived in the mail," Mr. Woodrow continued, "and it was dinner at a nice restaurant out Columbus way, and a gift certificate for this bed and breakfast inn nearby. The only catch was, we could only use it last night. After that date, it expired. So I said to Claudia, 'Why not?' Didn't I, sweetie?"

"Yes, that's what he said all right," said Mrs. Woodrow

with a little nod toward her husband. "He said 'Why not?' "

"Sort of a second honeymoon, I guess," said Jackie.

"Oh, I've lost track of how many honeymoons we've had in the last fifty-two years," said Ed. "This might've been eleven or twelve."

Mrs. Woodrow blushed becomingly.

Jackie allowed herself an inward sigh. What did it take, she wondered, to make a relationship stay this good for this many years? Whatever it was, she was beginning to be afraid none of the men she met had it. Or maybe it was Jackie who didn't have it. Either way, it looked like she was out of luck.

"Look, Ed," said Mrs. Woodrow, "there's a lot of people standing out in front of Franklin and Winnie's house. What's that all about, do you suppose?"

"Well, I hate to be the one to tell you," Jackie said, "but Franklin and Winnie's house was broken into last night. Your house is fine, though. No problem there," she hastened to assure them. "And we'd already moved all of Winnie's stuff out of the house, so the burglars didn't get anything."

"Oh, my goodness!" exclaimed Mrs. Woodrow, hands fluttering, "I've got to go and get a closer look!" And she was off down the sidewalk to the other side of the hedge where all the excitement was.

"I hope you'll forgive Claudia," said Ed Woodrow affectionately, smiling at his wife as she hurried off. "She's kind of a free spirit."

"Have you found out anything about the goldbacks yet?" Frances asked Jackie after they left Mr. Woodrow and continued to walk to their cars.

"I was just getting ready to look up some coin dealers when you called me this morning," said Jackie. "I guess we could go find a pay phone and call a few of them from there.''

"If you're quick about it," said Frances. "All this excitement has me starving to death. You're buying breakfast."

"This is an old goldback twenty-dollar bill," said Mr. Krause, Proprietor of The Coin Corner on West Seventh Avenue in downtown Palmer, Ohio. He held it up to the light coming in through the dusty windows of his little shop. Mr. Krause had been reluctant to quote a solid figure on the bill without laying eyes on it, so Jackie had driven the short distance between the pay phone and The Coin Corner to let him see it in the flesh, so to speak.

"It's in good condition, too," he said with admiration, "though one might wish it had been stored just a little more carefully." He looked up at Jackie over the tops of his glasses. "It would be worth more if it had been preserved better, of course. Sealed in a Mylar sleeve, for example, or wrapped in acid-free paper. Where on earth did you find it?"

"It was left to me by a relative," said Jackie. "A collector. I'm not thinking of parting with it right now, but I thought I'd find out what it would bring if I ever decided to sell it." Mr. Krause was the third coin dealer Jackie had gifted with this cover story this morning, and he was just as enthusiastic about the goldback as the first two.

Mr. Krause perused the contents of a high shelf behind the register, pulled down a thick, dog-eared paperback, and began riffling through its pages. Jackie looked around at the coin shop, with its walls covered with framed mint sets and commemoratives, and racks of tubes and jackets and albums for storing coins. Most of it looked as though it hadn't been dusted, or otherwise disturbed, for untold years.

"Here we are," said Mr. Krause when he had found the

entry he was searching for. "Well, if you decide to sell it to me, I'll give you forty dollars for it."

That was nearly half again what the last man had said, Jackie noted, but for the offer to roll off Mr. Krause's tongue that easily, Jackie figured the bill might be worth still more.

"That's very generous," she said. "I'll keep your offer in mind." She pulled gently on one end of the old twenty and Mr. Krause let go the other end reluctantly. "Do you see many of these in a year?" she asked him.

"Not any more," said Mr. Krause, shaking his head sadly. "Now and again an estate sale . . ." He gazed at the goldback until Jackie slipped it back into its envelope and into her purse. "Just let me know if you ever want to sell it," he said wistfully.

"You bet," Jackie replied.

She stopped at the door and turned back around to face Mr. Krause. "Just out of curiosity," she began, "if I had more than one of these, would your offer still be the same for each one?"

Mr. Krause cocked his head and raised his eyebrows. "You have more than one of them? Several? How many?"

"You've been very helpful, Mr. Krause. Thanks a million." Or a hundred and fifty thousand, anyway. She closed the door of the shop carefully behind her.

CHAPTER 18

Jackie and Frances sat in the red-upholstered back booth of Miranda's Healthy Stuff Café a tiny hole in the wall in one of the older and friendlier neighborhoods of downtown Palmer, and Jackie went over the case with her mother the way she had done with herself much earlier this morning.

She had covered most of the points that were still on her little yellow notes at home on the dining room table, including the connection between a severed right thumb and a guy called Lefty, by the time their orders arrived.

"Why didn't I think of that?" Frances wondered.

"That's what I said." Jackie slapped her forehead. " 'Duh,' as Peter would say."

"He'd be right, too," said Frances. "Well, now we know."

It was not yet ten A.M., but Jackie couldn't help thinking she'd already put in a full day, and she was unexpectedly hungry. She bit into her sandwich: Jack cheese, tomato, sprouts, cucumber, avocado, and red onion on sourdough wheat bread—a Miranda's tradition—and smiled. She really must make these at home sometime, if she could convince Miranda to sell her some of the homemade raspberry dressing that provided the finishing touch. She stifled a yawn with one hand as the waitress poured coffee.

"Up late?" Frances wanted to know, as if her daughter might still have a ten o'clock curfew at age thirty-eight.

"Not really," Jackie replied. "I went to bed a little while after I got home from Dwight Hockersmith's party last night."

"Boring," Frances proclaimed, not inaccurately. "It put me to sleep, too. So did the candidate, I'm afraid. And how about that Old Judge Hockersmith?" she inquired, laughing. "Shaking hands spreads germs, indeed. So does kissing, but no one ever stopped doing it for that reason."

"Somehow I can't see him kissing anyone, either," said Jackie with a smile. "In fact I wonder if Dwight might be adopted."

"No, they look too much alike," Frances observed. "But if you want to talk about dirty tricks of fate, what do you think of poor Franklin Swann ending up with a son like Dalton?"

Jackie shuddered. "I pity anyone who's related to Dalton. Except Claire," she decided after a moment. "I think she deserves him."

"They deserve one another," Frances agreed. She studied Jackie's outfit with interest. "You're certainly well turned out for someone who dressed to attend the scene of a burglary this morning, Jacqueline," she commented.

"Oh, this?" Jackie indicated the silk shirt with a dismissive gesture. "Peter and I are going out later to meet some friends. Acquaintances, really. A dog trainer and his daughter."

Jackie must have let some slight facial expression get by in spite of her usual Herculean effort to conceal any newsworthy emotion from her mother, because Frances was on her like ducks on a bug, as her Grandfather Cooley would have said.

"Do tell me more about this dog trainer," Frances said, leaning over her coffee cup toward Jackie, and smiling what she doubtless assumed was a subtle little smile.

"Oh, nothing to tell, really," Jackie said with a wave of her hand. "He moved here from California with his teenage daughter, took over Mel Sweeten's old kennels, and started a new business there about three months ago. His name is Tom Cusack."

"An Irishman. Good start," Frances commented, nodding her head.

"That's not what you said when I brought Cooper home," Jackie retorted.

"The only thing Irish about Cooper Walsh was his last name," Frances snorted. "If you hadn't been in such a hurry to marry someone, you'd have been able to see that behind that handsome face and all that charm, there really wasn't anything to Cooper at all that should have captured the interest of an intelligent young woman like you."

The waitress arrived to refill their cups, and Frances was silent for a few moments while she fussed over them, then left a check on the table. "You know it never mattered to me in the least if the man you married was Irish or not. He could have been Italian, or German, or Lithuanian, for God's sake."

"But not English," Jackie hastened to point out, resisting the urge to smile.

"Hopefully not, please God," said Frances with a perfectly straight face, "but wherever his folks came from, I wanted him to be a real man—a real person, not just a good-looking piece of cardboard with a lot of ambition and a high-paying job."

"Well, you were several steps ahead of me on that one, Mother," Jackie admitted. "It took me a long time to figure out just how little there was to Cooper, and a long time after that to be honest enough with myself to admit it."

And another long time before she could bring herself to leave him, and only then because she found out he was cheating on her. She'd wanted to hold things together for Peter's sake, but that had been as big a mistake as marrying him in the first place. So many years wasted . . . but that was then.

"So is this one any better?"

"Oh, for heaven's sake, Mother, how would I know? I only met him yesterday."

"I knew I'd marry your father the instant I laid eyes on him," said Frances. "There was just something about him. . . ."

Her voice trailed off, and she gazed off into the distance for a moment, remembering. Jackie remembered her father, too, as a person with a special combination of intellectual and emotional gifts the likes of which she'd never seen in another man. Jackie put a hand over her mother's. "Dad was an exceptional man, Mother. I know that."

Frances looked at Jackie again. "Exceptional, yes. But not singular. There are lots and lots of good men out there, my dear, and a few truly special ones. Don't be afraid to reach out and grab one of them if you happen to see him going by."

"Okay. I won't." Jackie put down the portion of her sandwich she wasn't prepared to finish. She caught a look from Frances and headed her off at the pass. "No, I'm not going to clean my plate, Mother. Cleaning my plate when I'm not hungry any more makes me gain weight. Gaining weight makes me depressed. Being depressed makes me irritate the hell out of you."

"Oh, all right. I guess you're a big girl now," her mother conceded.

Wow, thought Jackie, imagine that. Only thirty-eight and a big girl already. Things were definitely looking up in her life. "Say, isn't this the day Barney Dorfmeier was supposed to be back from his out-of-town trip?" she asked her mother.

"If this is Saturday it is," Frances said. "I think I've lost track. This has certainly been some week, hasn't it?"

"That's one way to put it," Jackie admitted with a sigh.

She successfully resisted the urge to remind her mother that it would have been a perfectly ordinary week without her insisting on poking her nose into other people's business. "Do you have his telephone number with you?"

"It's right here," said Frances, reaching into her handbag and handing Jackie a piece of paper with the number written on it in her elegant, girls'-school handwriting. The nuns had been insistent on penmanship as a prerequisite of social success, and Frances Cooley had been their star pupil. And star troublemaker, too. You could get a single ounce of Irish whiskey into her and hear all the stories.

"I'll just go to the pay phone and give him a call then," said Jackie. She walked back through a set of swinging doors to the dark, narrow hallway between the restrooms, and dug some change out of her pockets for the phone.

Barney Dorfmeier's granddaughter, Mrs. Batcheler, answered the phone. "Yes, Grandpa got back just fine," she reported, "and he's already got company today, an old friend." She remembered that Frances had called previously, and that they wanted to talk to her grandfather about Franklin and Winnie Swann. "Grandpa just loved Mr. Swann," said Mrs. Batcheler fondly. "He was so saddened by his death. Is Mrs. Swann all right? Nothing's happened to her, I hope."

"No, she's fine," Jackie assured her. "Do you think Mr. Dorfmeier will have a few minutes to talk to us this morning?"

"I'm sure he will, but why don't you let me go and ask him? Just to be sure, I mean."

When she came back she reported that her grandfather would be happy to have them visit any time in the next hour. After that it would be time for his nap, and he never missed his nap. "Grandpa's not getting any younger, you know. Ninety-one last month."

"We can be there in twenty minutes," Jackie told her. "Just give me your address."

•   •   •

Mrs. Batcheler met them at the imposing double doors of
a large, red brick house with incongruous white columns,
trim painted a blinding white, and a lawn like a small golf
course. A mailbox shaped like a little red barn bore the
name *Batcheler* in black wrought-iron letters.

The house was in an unfamiliar part of town, much
newer and much ritzier than the usual neighborhoods in
which either Jackie or Frances were used to finding their
way around. Without a current map of Palmer and its suburbs, it had taken them the better part of forty-five minutes
to find the Batcheler residence in the maze of winding
drives and annoying cul-de-sacs that had been drawn out,
Jackie was sure, by some gleefully sadistic planner with a
Spirograph toy.

"Grandpa's friend left a few minutes ago," said Mrs.
Batcheler, a small, pale woman in her late forties, "and
Grandpa's up in his room. This is such a busy day for him,
but I know he'll want to talk to you about Mr. Swann. I'll
just go tell him you've arrived. Won't be a minute," she
called behind her as she trotted up a winding staircase to
the second floor.

A few moments later there was a shrill scream from the
top of the stairs. Jackie and Frances started upstairs, but
before they could get very far, Mrs. Batcheler came running
out of one of the bedrooms, hands clutching her hair. "He's
dead!" she shrieked. "Grandpa's dead!"

CHAPTER 19

Jackie raced up the stairs and Frances followed, a bit more slowly, behind her. Mrs. Batcheler was standing in the doorway, eyes wide, staring at the old man who lay on the antique four-poster bed, pale blue eyes staring blankly at the ceiling.

Jackie stepped past her into the room. She was pretty sure he was dead all right, but she picked up his hand and felt for a pulse, just to be sure. The skin of his wrist was dry and a little cool, and she could feel no heartbeat there. She felt the sides of his neck and the hollow of his throat. Nothing. No sign of breath or movement, either. His eyes were already beginning to film over. She stepped away from him and turned back to Mrs. Batcheler.

"He was alive when you talked to me on the phone a little while ago," she said.

Mrs. Batcheler sniffed, reached into her dress pocket for a neatly ironed white handkerchief, wiped her nose, and sniffed again. "The doctor's been saying for over a year now that his heart could go at any time, without warning. That was the way Grandpa wanted to die—quickly. No lingering." Her voice broke, and she sobbed quietly into the handkerchief.

"Well, he got his wish," said Frances, patting Mrs.

Batcheler gently on the shoulder. "We should all be so lucky. Close his eyes, Jacqueline."

Jackie stared at her mother for a moment, but Frances only nodded in Barney Dorfmeier's direction and led Mrs. Batcheler out of the room.

Hesitantly, Jackie approached the bed again and reached out a hand toward Barney Dorfmeier's face. "Rest in peace, Mr. Dorfmeier," she said, trembling just a little as she brushed her fingers over his eyelids. His lashes tickled her palm, making her shudder slightly. "But in the interest of honesty, I have to say your timing was lousy," she added. "Sorry."

"It's like I've been telling my film class," said Jackie to her mother. "There was a feeling in the air back in the twenties that was less than law-abiding." Jackie and Frances were back at Miranda's having another cup of coffee. Jackie wasn't sure they needed any more caffeine after their unnerving experience at Mrs. Batcheler's house, but they needed *something*, and it was much too early in the day to start drinking.

"You had Prohibition, of course, which had otherwise honest people breaking the law on a regular basis, and kind of enjoying the sensation. Things you used to do or not do without thinking—buying liquor, going out for a drink— were suddenly forbidden, so most people felt like they had to do them with a vengeance, and that made them criminals automatically."

"Nothing sweeter than forbidden fruit," Frances agreed. "Though I understand bathtub gin was pretty awful. Your Grandfather Cooley used to buy Irish whiskey that had been brought in through Canada, but it cost him dearly, of course."

"Supply and demand," Jackie agreed. "When you can't get something readily its value increases, and that extra money had to line someone's pockets. Having something as common as alcohol made illegal was a golden opportunity for organized crime, too.''

''Your Grandfather Cooley used to say he thought the whole thing was a set-up. An artificial industry, he called it. The gangsters made millions, and crooked cops and judges, and who knows—even Congressmen—got a cut of every dime.''

''And the gangsters were kind of glorified,'' Jackie went on, ''you know, the way they were written up in the papers, and talked about by people on the street. The gangster movies were just getting started, and I don't even want to get into a discussion of whether they encouraged it or only reported on it, but the feeling in the air—the *zeitgeist*, I guess you'd call it—was pretty bold. Even defiant.''

''I know what you mean,'' said Frances. ''I grew up on my parent's stories about those days. They said guys like John Dillinger and Pretty Boy Floyd were heroes to a lot of people. Folks followed stories about what they were up to like it was a rousing good serial. And the law was as corrupt as the gangsters in those days, if you believe your Grandfather Cooley, except at least the gangsters were honest about it.''

''It still doesn't explain why three young men decided to rob a bank, does it?'' Jackie sighed.

''It doesn't explain it,'' Frances said, ''but it puts it into a perspective, sort of.''

''And two of them were, as far as we know, law-abiding citizens for the rest of their lives. It doesn't exactly fit the profile of your average bank robber, does it?''

''And then there's the third man,'' said Frances. ''Who the hell is he?''

Jackie told her mother about showing Cosmo Gordon a photograph of the thumb Jake had found at Winnie's. ''Cosmo said the person who lost that thumb could have died of their wounds if they weren't treated promptly, but Winnie says Lefty was still alive the last she heard. I think

Lefty might have gone on to lead a perfectly respectable life just like the other two, maybe even right here in Palmer.''

''So all we have to do is find all the ninety-year-old men in town and get them to take their hands out of their pockets.'' She stopped, noticing the expression on Jackie's face. ''What did I say?'' she asked.

''Ohmigod, Mother, we just met a ninety-year-old man last night. . . .''

''. . . who had his hands in his pockets,'' Frances finished for her. ''How did we miss it?''

''Because it was Old Judge Hockersmith,'' said Jackie, sitting back in her seat, heart pounding. ''Whew! Talk about your respectable life! No wonder Franklin had to have something on him. 'Lefty' had a lot to lose if he were exposed, even after the statute of limitations ran out on the robbery.''

''I knew there was something I didn't like about that old codger,'' Frances muttered.

''And I knew I'd seen him somewhere before. Now I remember where it must have been. He walked by me in front of Winnie's house the first day we were there. He was wearing black gloves.''

''I think the old fella who was going by the second time we were at the house was wearing gloves, too,'' said Frances. ''I'll bet you anything he was keeping an eye on the place.''

''And I'll bet he's the one who ripped it to shreds last night, too. He must have gone there after the party. First he saw me outside Winnie's house, then he found out I knew Winnie, and Dwight said he went to school with Franklin Swann.''

''I don't know, Jacqueline—the old geezer might be spry for ninety-something, but whoever hacked out those walls and pried up those floorboards had to put some serious muscle into it.''

"So he had help," said Jackie.

"If he didn't, he's *really* feeling his age today."

"Dwight?"

"Possibly," Frances allowed.

"Better and better. If anyone found out about the Judge's felonious youth, Dwight's mayoral campaign wouldn't stand a snowball's chance. He'd have more to protect than his father does, when you come right down to it—he's almost sixty years younger, with a lot more future ahead of him." Marcella Jacobs would love to get her hands on this, Jackie thought, but there was something more important at stake than just digging dirt.

"Jacqueline Shannon Costello, what are you thinking?" Frances demanded as she studied Jackie's face across the table.

"Whether or not I should call Evan Stillman and tell him what's been going on."

"You can't be serious!"

"Mother, the bank robbery's one thing—it happened seventy years ago and no one cares anymore except Judge Hockersmith and possibly Dwight. But the burglary's a nice, fresh crime, and we have important evidence about who may have done it."

"And revealing that evidence means revealing the existence of Winnie's money," Frances reminded her, unnecessarily.

"Maybe I can put that part off for a while," said Jackie. "I can tell Evan that Judge Hockersmith was looking for money he thought was hidden in the house—that's only the truth. The money is evidence in a case the law has no interest in, so we can't get into any serious legal trouble for knowing about it and not telling."

"He's not going to be exactly overjoyed about it just the same," Frances warned her.

"No, but all he can do is yell at us—he can't arrest us," Jackie said. "I don't think he can, anyway. I can also tell

him what we've been told about the bank robbery if it will
help explain Judge Hockersmith's motive for the burglary,
but the only witness we have that Winnie's money has any
connection to it is Winnie, and when it comes right down
to it . . .''

"Winnie's elevator doesn't go all the way to the top
floor," said Frances. "So anything she said about the
money wouldn't be taken seriously anyway. And Judge
Hockersmith isn't likely to admit to knowing anything
about it in the first place."

"And we've taken the money out of the house. . . .''

"So Dalton and Claire have no proof it was ever *in* the
house. This is a pretty tangled plan, darling daughter."

"It hurts my brain just to think of it," Jackie admitted.
"I hope I'm not missing anything obvious or breaking any
major laws I haven't thought of yet. I still wish I knew why
they robbed the damn bank in the first place."

"Maybe Barney Dorfmeier could have explained it to
us," said Frances, "but we got there a few minutes too
late."

"Too late! Ohmigod, what time is it?" Jackie looked at
her wrist, but she'd forgotten to put on her watch today, in
her hurry to get over to Winnie's house after her mother's
phone call.

Frances checked her own watch. "It's about twenty
minutes until two," she said.

"I've got to run, Mother. Peter will never speak to me
again if I'm late. I'll call Evan just as soon as I get home
this afternoon." She grabbed her car keys, reached into her
pocket, and pulled out a few crumpled dollar bills, which
she tossed onto the table.

"I'm going to see Winnie tomorrow," said Frances.
"Care to come with me? Maybe you could bring Jake
along, too."

"Sounds great. Call me." Jackie hurried from the café
and down the sidewalk to her car. She should be able to

make it home in a bit less than twenty minutes if traffic was kind.

Traffic was a little less than kind, but a bit of moderate speeding and a bit of creative driving got her parked in front of her townhouse on Isabella Lane at a minute or so before two. Peter was waiting patiently, for a teenager, at the dining room table, Jake curled up at his feet, head resting on his paws, his leather lead close by on the carpet. Both gave her mildly accusing looks as she burst in the front door.

"Told you I'd make it," she said, only a little out of breath. "You two ready to go?"

CHAPTER 20

"It's very likely Jake has had some search training in order to work as a police service dog," said Tom to Jackie and Peter. "It may very well have been search-and-detain training rather than search-and-rescue, but both use the same basic tracking and trailing skills."

"Search-and-detain? You mean like looking for bad guys and holding them?" Peter inquired.

"Exactly," said Tom. "Police dogs sometimes have to run after fleeing suspects, and find them by the scent they leave behind. If the dog gets out of sight of the officer he's working with during the pursuit, he has to know what to do when he apprehends the suspect, without being supervised."

"What would that be, just out of curiosity?" Jackie asked.

"Well, there's a couple of different schools of thought on that, but most dogs these days are trained to hold the suspect by intimidation—you know, barking, growling, that sort of thing. They won't bite unless the suspect does one of the things they've been trained to respond to, but if he does one of those things, they'll bite like they mean business, and hold on until the officer calls them off."

He patted Jake's head affectionately as he went on. "If

the suspect pulled out a gun or a knife, say, the dog would attack the arm that held the weapon, even if the officer wasn't there to give the command. If the suspect tried to run, the dog would bring him down with a bite, maybe to the back of the leg.''

Peter looked proud. ''That all sounds pretty smart, doesn't it?''

''Well, Jake's no loser in the brains department, I suspect,'' Tom told him. ''The proof of that is that he went all the way through the training and was accepted for police service, and did his job well, I'm told.'' He smiled at Jackie, then turned back to Peter. ''Shepherds are pretty smart as a breed,'' he said, ''but even so, not every shepherd has what it takes to do the work. Your Jake's something special, all right.''

Jake seemed to accept all this praise in stride, sitting very still, with only his huge black ears moving this way and that as he caught the sounds of birdsong.

''What I'd like to do today,'' said Tom, ''is to put Jake through a basic searching exercise, just to remind him of what he probably already knows.''

''So what do you want us to do?'' Jackie asked. The two adults and the two teenagers were a few miles outside town in a pleasant wooded area with a clear stream flowing by, and a few scattered granite boulders. It would be pleasant enough just to sit and enjoy the warm breeze coming through the trees, but Tom had brought them here to put Jake through his paces.

''Well, the first thing we need is a scent article,'' said Tom. ''Peter, why don't you give me that sweatshirt? Better yet, hand it to your mother. We don't want so many scents on it that Jake gets confused about who he's supposed to be finding. Jake's already familiar with your mother's scent, and he won't be thrown off by it.''

Peter untied his red Palmer Arts School sweatshirt from around his waist and handed it to Jackie, who bundled it up under one arm. "We're going to take Jake down the trail over there out of sight," said Tom.

"Peter," he continued, looking around at their surroundings, "I'd like you to walk up to the top of that little rise and sit down for a minute. Then get up and touch that tree." He indicated a tall, spreading oak near the spot where Peter was supposed to sit. "After that, just take off down the other side of the hill, but be sure to make a lot of twists and turns and circles—don't just go in a straight line. Reach out and touch something whenever you feel like it."

"Is that it?" Peter asked.

"Just about. Keep walking for about twenty minutes, then stop and wait for us." He turned to Jackie. "Let's get out of sight, so we know Jake's following a scent trail and not just going where he saw Peter go."

"You want me to start now?" Peter asked.

"Just as soon as we get around that bend in the path, and out of sight," said Tom.

"Can I go with Peter?" Grania asked casually.

Jackie could see the corners of Tom's mouth turning up in the beginnings of a smile, but he managed to keep a reasonably straight face. "If it's okay with Peter, it's okay with me," he told her.

Grania turned to Peter. "Is it okay if I come along with you?"

"Uh, sure," Peter replied.

"That's my son, the slick ladies' man," Jackie said, pitching her voice low enough that Tom was the only one who could hear her.

Tom smiled. "Let's get going," he said. They walked down the winding trail and were out of sight within a hundred yards of the two teenagers.

"Now what?" Jackie wanted to know.

"Now we give them a twenty-minute head start," said Tom, checking his watch. "So we might as well find a spot to sit down and relax."

Jackie sat down on the ground with her back to a sturdy oak tree. Tom sat a couple of feet away. Jake lay down between them with a contented grunt, and put his head between his paws, though his ears still stood at attention. Tom unclipped the lead from his collar and placed it beside him.

It was a beautiful late spring day, and Jackie had no objection to sitting still for a few minutes and just enjoying the scenery and Tom Cusack's company. Worrying about illicit currency and chasing after aging bank robbers with her mother had taken a lot out of her the past week, and finding Barney Dorfmeier dead only a few hours before had put the finishing touches on it. She could only hope that the worst was over. She rolled up the sleeves of her shirt.

"Ouch," said Tom. "What're the bandages for?"

Jackie held up her arms. "For klutziness," she said. "I took a spill the other day."

"Nothing like a little excitement in an otherwise boring day," said Tom.

Jackie didn't exactly know what to say to that—she wasn't about to get into the story of why she and Jake were racing for possession of unburied human remains, as Cosmo called the thumb.

She wondered what Tom would think of some of her extracurricular activities; they'd only had one real conversation, and they hadn't yet gotten onto the subject of her occasional detective work. It seemed to Jackie there was plenty of time to bring up some of the more unorthodox aspects of her life when they knew each other a bit better.

"It looks like your son has a real case on my daughter," Tom remarked.

"I'd say that's pretty accurate," Jackie replied. "He gets this sort of beatific look whenever I mention her."

"Well, Grania tries to be cool about it, but I can tell she likes him," said Tom. "He's the only boy she ever talks about at home, and that's always a sign with teenage girls.

At least it is with Grania, and she seems pretty typical of the species.''

"Well, if you don't mind me saying it, I think she's a pretty exceptional teenage girl. Exceptionally pretty, too.''

Tom blushed just a bit. "Thanks. She must take after her mother in that department.''

"Actually, except for her coloring, I think she looks a lot like you.'' It was Jackie's turn to blush as she realized what she was saying. Too late to call the words back, but what the hell? She met Tom's look as steadily as possible. "She's got your eyes for sure.''

The eyes in question, deep blue and pleasantly large, with a fringe of dark lashes, were fixed on her face for a long moment before his gaze dropped back to the ground in front of him. "She's a great kid. It'd be a lot lonelier around the house without her.''

"Well, they all leave eventually,'' said Jackie. "And when they reach this age, I'm told, the years become a blur. It's something a parent probably ought to keep in mind.''

"You're right.'' Tom shook his head. "I can't believe how fast she's grown, and how grown-up she seems sometimes. Then at other times she's just a little girl. I guess she's still figuring out which she really is—a child or an adult.''

"Hey, I'm still figuring that one out,'' said Jackie with a smile, "and I'm close enough to forty to smell the birthday candles.''

"I don't think women really start getting interesting until they're nearly forty,'' said Tom, looking up at her again.

Jackie wondered if that meant he thought she was interesting. She decided it did, but she didn't know what to say to that. Maybe changing the subject was called for here. "So how much time do we have left before we have to go tracking?'' she asked him, hoping she didn't sound as lame as she felt.

Tom checked his watch. "Another fifteen minutes. Getting bored?"

Jackie drew up her knees and put her chin on them. The warm spring sun was coming through a gap in the branches of the tree above them and warming her back. "Nope. I could sit here all day." She sighed with contentment. "Well, maybe not *all* day, but a long time, anyhow."

"Yeah, it's pretty nice out here, all right. So, when was the last time you got out of town and looked at a tree that wasn't planted by the City of Palmer?" Tom asked.

Jackie thought about this for a moment. "Can't remember. Too long." She shrugged. "I guess I'm just a city girl at heart."

"It's always good to get away from your environment now and again, whatever it is," Tom mused. "I lived out in the country for eleven years during the time I was married to Marcy—that's Grania's mother—but every now and again I had to go into the city for a weekend to recharge my batteries.

"After that we moved to San Francisco. We lived there for three years, and it's a great place—like no other city I've ever seen—but every few months I'd have to head for the hills to keep my sanity intact. Guess I just can't make up my mind."

"No, it sounds like you have a good sense of balance. Very unusual, I'd say."

"Well, thanks. I kind of like being unusual. There's altogether too much usual in the world. I get the feeling you enjoy being different, too."

You have no idea, Jackie thought to herself, but resisted saying it out loud. She was just a little afraid for Tom Cusack to find out too soon just how strange she really was. She wondered how many of the women he'd been interested in had been centrally involved in a dozen murders, pursued by knife- and gun-wielding crime suspects, and were better known by their local police departments than most lifelong criminals. "I've always been a bit unconventional, I guess," is what she did say, finally. "Peter's father never knew what to make of me, that's for sure."

"What's he like? Peter's father?"

"Extremely conventional," said Jackie, shaking her head involuntarily the way she always did when she talked about Cooper Walsh. "Upstanding citizen of suburbia. Successful businessman, low-handicap golfer, ladies' man extraordinaire."

Tom nodded. "I see."

Jackie realized she had revealed a bit more than she'd meant to about the problems between her and her first husband. It had just come out, probably because Tom made her feel so comfortable. She couldn't recall too many moments of comfort in her marriage. Unless you counted a sort of numb contentment that masked a lot of anxiety and anger, and she didn't, not since she'd woken up and realized she had to get out of her marriage if she was going to stay sane.

"So what made you choose Palmer?" she asked Tom, still seeking a reasonably safe area to take their conversation. "Ohio is a long way from California, in more ways than one."

"When the kennels came up for sale there was an ad in a national dog-training magazine," said Tom. "I'd been working for other people's businesses training dogs for half my life, and I really wanted my own kennels, but you wouldn't believe the price of real estate in Northern California. I'd been saving up, but then there was the divorce. . . ."

"Yeah, they can be expensive," Jackie agreed. "Sometimes," she added with a smile, "they cost a lot of money, too."

Tom laughed. "You've got that right," he said ruefully. "So how do you like Palmer so far?"

"A lot," he said. "It's a big enough place to offer a variety of things to do, but not too big to get to know in a fairly short time. It's not San Francisco, exactly, but it looks better than Los Angeles, and it smells better than New York."

Jackie smiled at that. She'd seen L.A. and smelled New York. Tom was right on both counts.

"In San Francisco I was into the Irish scene—you know—traditional bands, *seisiuns*. There's a lot of that going on out there."

"Not much of that in Palmer, as far as I know."

"Well, not as many Irish, proportionately, in the midwest as in New York or San Francisco, but I did find a place in the city that has great music."

"Really? Where?"

"It's called Bridget O'Malley's."

"As in 'young Bridget O'Malley who threw my heart away'?" Jackie asked, quoting the English translation of the words to an old Irish song.

"That must be where they got it," Tom said. "It's on Second Avenue near Illinois Street."

"That's not that far from where I live," said Jackie, shaking her head. "How'd I miss it?"

"I think it's new. The beauty of it is, though, it looks old. Battered old long wooden tables and benches, a big old antique bar, that sort of thing."

"And a television where they show the Gaelic Football matches on weekends?"

"You know, I'm beginning to suspect you *are* Irish. I wondered if you'd only married an Irishman."

"Jacqueline Shannon Costello," said Jackie. "And my mother's a Cooley. I'm named for her father, Jack Cooley, and her mother, Julia Shannon."

"Good credentials, those," he admitted. "My mother's a Madden. How do you suppose all these folks from a tiny little island keep finding one another on this great big continent?''

"Just lucky? Well, not in the case of Cooper and I." Jackie mentally berated herself for getting back on the subject of Cooper Walsh. She thought she'd put her unhappy marriage far behind her, but lately it seemed to be haunting her a lot.

"It's been years since I heard any good trad music," she said, back on a safer subject. "Well, I've got a pretty good collection of CDs at home, but it's been a long time since I went to a *seisiun.*"

"I could talk traditional bands all afternoon," said Tom as he checked his watch again, "but unfortunately, it looks like it's time to go find the kids. Come on, Jake," he said, clipping Jake's leather lead onto his collar and patting the shepherd's head, "It's time to get to work, old boy.''

CHAPTER 21

Once Tom had offered Peter's sweatshirt—held out on the end of a stick to minimize any extra scents—to Jake to sniff at, he said, "Go to work, Jake!" and Jake began walking around and sniffing the air eagerly. After a few moments his ears shot up and his body went tense for just an instant; then he took off, tugging hard at his lead, feet scrambling in the loose dirt and leaves on the ground.

Tom seemed to have expected this, and wasn't taken off balance, but began to walk rapidly behind Jake. Jackie scrambled to keep up with them as they hurried back up the path in the direction they had come from twenty minutes before. She was glad she'd worn her hiking boots, but it had been too long since the last time she'd laced them up, and she was soon out of breath and lagging behind.

Tom slowed the big dog down a bit and gave Jackie a chance to come up even with them.

"Sorry I'm such a wimp," Jackie apologized, breathing hard. "I never used to be this out of shape."

"It sneaks up on you," Tom said sympathetically. "And then, too, Jake's pretty enthusiastic about all this," he added. "I think he's going to give us quite a workout."

"What's he doing?" she asked, indicating Jake's eager

scenting of the air. "Do you think he smells Peter already?"

"Yeah, he can smell him, but he doesn't know exactly where he is yet. Don't worry, though—he *will*, soon enough."

"Are you sure he can find them? They could be a mile away by now!"

"Well, you have to remember that the worst dog nose out there—the one on your Aunt Minnie's Pomeranian, say—is still maybe a million times better at scenting than yours or mine," Tom told her as Jake strained at the lead and tried to get him to walk faster. "With a dog like Jake here or with a top-of-the-line bloodhound, say, we may be talking about scenting abilities a hundred million times better than a human nose."

"That's pretty good, all right," Jackie commented with appreciation.

"That's one way of putting it," said Tom. "Pretty amazing might be another way. We could put our noses right on someone's footprint and not smell a thing but some dirt, but catching a trailing scent near where someone was twenty minutes ago is kindergarten work for a trained search dog."

Jake continued to sniff the air, zigzagging back and forth as he went, but always heading in the same general direction.

"Why is he going sideways like that?" Jackie wanted to know.

"The path he's following now is sort of defining the area of the airborne scent," said Tom, sketching Jake's movements in the air with his hand. "You can imagine the scent dissipating from where Peter started in a sort of cone shape, narrower near where he laid down the scent patch by stopping under the tree, and wider nearer to us, because the scent has spread out further the longer it's been since it was laid down."

He followed along, and Jackie followed behind him, as Jake's meandering pattern grew narrower and narrower near the top of the hill where Tom had first told Peter to sit down and wait for a minute before he walked away.

"This zigzagging thing he's doing is just going back and forth between the boundaries of that scent cone," said Tom, "but he's always headed for where the scent is strongest, and all other things being equal, that's going to be where Peter actually stood, or sat, or walked."

"What would make that any different?" Jackie wanted to know.

"Oh, the wind, or rain, or the relative dampness or dryness of the ground, or whether it was in sun or shade—things like that."

"So does something damp hold scent better than something dry?"

"Usually. Running water's an obvious exception, of course. And a shady spot holds better than a sunny one. There are a lot of different conditions you have to keep in mind," Tom told her. "Of course, Jake doesn't have to think about any of this the way we do. All he has to do is sniff."

As they reached the place where the four of them had stood before the two teenagers went off in a different direction, Jake put his nose to the ground and whined, then pulled Tom off in the direction that Tom had told Peter to take. He showed a lot of interest in the spot where Peter had sat down, and also at the nearby tree Tom had told Peter to touch. Then he led them down the other side of the hill, staying right over Peter and Grania's shoe prints most of the time, but occasionally veering off to the left a few feet.

"He's not actually following their footprints, is he?" Jackie asked Tom.

"Not the way you or I would," Tom replied. "Humans track mostly with their eyes, so those shoe prints would be

an important clue to us. They don't mean a thing to Jake—
all he cares about is what he smells. That's why he's wandering away from the prints sometimes—there's been a
breeze blowing in from that direction,'' Tom pointed off to
their right, ''and it's blown some of the scent away from
the track, the path Peter actually walked. The longer it's
been since a scent was laid down, the more of it will have
drifted off.''

A little further down the trail, Jake came to a pile of
granite boulders and seemed to lose the scent. He sniffed
here and there, growing more and more frustrated. After a
few moments Tom led him over to a depression between
two of the boulders. Jake took one sniff and was back on
track, pulling Tom along behind him, snuffling at the
ground near where the shoe prints picked back up again.

''It was pretty smart of Peter to go over those rocks,''
said Tom. ''Rocks don't hold scent as well as dirt or veg-
etation.''

''But you showed Jake where to pick up the scent
again,'' said Jackie.

''A dog only knows what he knows, no matter how smart
he is,'' said Tom with a shrug. ''Jake knew he'd lost the
scent trail, but I knew that scent tends to pool in low places.
Whatever scent was on those rocks, it'd be strongest in a
depression like that.''

''So the handler has to be smarter than the dog,'' Jackie
commented with a grin.

Tom grinned back. ''Well, at least he has to know something about scent trails and the forces that work on them.
Jake's still got the edge when it comes to dog smarts.''

Jake followed the track scent a while longer, up and
down a couple of low hills and through some thick stands
of trees, while Jackie and Tom followed along. Then he
looked up suddenly and went into his alert posture again.
He pulled hard against his collar. They followed, Tom pull-

ing on the lead and slowing him down a bit as he tried to
break into a run.

"He's got a good airborne scent trail now," said Tom
over his shoulder to Jackie. "I think the kids aren't too far
away now." Sure enough, as they came over the crest of
a low rise, they saw Peter and Grania sitting down in the
shade of a tree, sharing a drink from a water bottle.

The teenagers waved when they saw their parents and
Jake coming toward them. Jake was nearly tearing the lead
out of Tom's hand now, and when he looked back over his
shoulder as if to hurry them up, Tom gave him a hand
signal that stopped him in his tracks. He lay down obedi-
ently at Tom's feet.

"Wow," said Jackie with admiration. "You're going to
have to teach me that one. How did you know that would
work on Jake?"

"I didn't, really. But most police dogs are trained to
hand signals, and I figured Jake would remember." He
leaned down to ruffle the fur around Jake's neck, while Jake
looked at him alertly, waiting patiently for permission to
get back up and run to Peter. "You did good, Jake," said
Tom.

He reached into his pocket, pulled out a brown cube, and
offered it to Jake. Jake wolfed it down happily. "Dried
liver," said Tom. "Dogs love it. Okay, Jake. You can go
now."

He unclipped the lead and Jake got up and trotted over
to the two teenagers, who greeted him with hugs and
whoops of delight. "Did you see that, Mom? He followed
our trail. Jake's a search dog!"

Tom stood up. Jackie crossed her arms in front of her
and cocked her head. "You carry liver around in your
pocket?"

"Well, not when I'm going out to dinner with a beautiful
woman," he replied. "Though it'd come in handy if they
were slow with the appetizers." He grinned and blushed as

he wiped his hands on his jeans. "So would you like to?"

"Snack on dried liver?" Jackie inquired with a straight face. "No, I don't think so. Sorry."

Tom smiled and blushed. "I meant, would you like to go to dinner?"

"Oh, that. Sure. When did you have in mind?"

"I was thinking about tonight."

CHAPTER 22

"Hey, Mom," said Peter casually as he got up from his place under the tree. "Remember that huge favor you owe me?"

Jackie remembered Peter's courageous expedition into the dark heart of his bedroom closet the previous day to retrieve the instant camera she needed to get a picture of the severed thumb. "How could I forget?" she asked him, pretty certain what was coming next. "Have you figured out how to call it in yet?"

"Well, I wouldn't call this a *huge* favor, exactly," Peter hedged.

"Just extra-large, then?"

"Not that big, either. Medium-sized."

"Like if I do this, whatever it is, I'll still owe you?"

"Kinda like that."

"We'll see. What do you need?"

"Well, there's a Bruce Lee triple feature tonight at the Sofia," said Peter, looking over at Grania, who got up and came over to stand near her father. "We were talking about going, but it starts in a little less than an hour. Do you think you could take us, and then pick us up at midnight when the last movie's over?"

"That's possible, but I'm not the only one who needs to approve this plan."

"Daddy?" Grania looked at Tom.

"Well, I don't know, Grania. Jackie and I have plans of our own for the evening," said Tom, feigning uncertainty.

"That's perfect!" Grania exclaimed. "We'll be at the movies and out of your way until midnight. How about it, Dad?"

"Okay, I know a losing battle when I see one. I guess it's all right with me if it's all right with Jackie," he said. "I need to get back to the kennels so I can send Joseph home and lock up for the night."

"I think I can handle a little light chauffeur duty," said Jackie, "but first I have to drop Jake off at the house, and you guys will have to have something to eat besides popcorn and chocolate."

"Okay, but we'll need to hurry if we're going to get there before *Enter the Dragon* starts. Can we grab some takeout?"

"It'll have to be healthy takeout," Jackie warned. "Vine Ripe Grill?" She named a place near the Sofia, the old renovated movie palace downtown where the triple feature was showing. "We can get you a couple of pita pockets, and you can wolf them down on the way to the Sofia."

"Okay, only let's get going, Mom," said Peter impatiently. He and Grania piled into the back seat of Jackie's Blazer, after letting Jake in the rear door. Jackie tossed Peter's sweatshirt into the back seat. It landed on Peter's head. He grinned as he pulled it off and tossed it onto the floor.

"What do you say we meet at Guido's on West Ohio and Fourteenth at a little after six?" Tom inquired. "You like Italian?"

"I adore it. I adore Guido's especially."

"Do you even adore the Frank Sinatra and Perry Como

records they play nonstop over the loudspeakers?'' Tom asked, cracking a smile.

"Oh, I can tune them out," Jackie assured him. "After a while they even have a strange sort of appeal. Part of the genuine Italian-American atmosphere."

Tom looked at her.

"Okay, ear plugs help."

"I'll try to remember to bring some," he said.

It only took a few moments for Jackie and Peter, working more or less cooperatively, to leave Jake fresh food and water and lock up the yard. When they got back inside, Grania stood in the high-ceilinged living room, staring at the old movie posters that lined the walls. "This is such a cool place!" she exclaimed.

"You'll have to come back when Peter and I have time to give you the full tour," said Jackie.

A few minutes later they had pulled up in front of the Vine Ripe Grill. A dark gray German import pulled in behind them, and someone honked a horn.

Jackie turned around. Angela Hockersmith was waving at her from behind the wheel of the other car. "I didn't know you liked to eat here, too!" she said, sticking her head out the side window of her car as Jackie got out of the Blazer.

"Just grabbing some quick takeout before I run the kids over to the Sofia for a movie," said Jackie. "Sorry I can't stop and chat, but time is not on my side right now."

"Oh, that's okay," said Angela. "We seem to be running into one another a lot lately—I'm sure I'll see you again soon. Enjoy your dinner!"

"Thanks." Jackie ran inside as Angela's car pulled away from the curb.

Dinner at Guido's was the most fun Jackie could remember having in months. Between her favorite fettucine with ar-

tichoke hearts and mushrooms, Guido's wonderful soft
breadsticks, and Tom Cusack's very pleasant company, she
could almost overlook the honey-voiced crooners on the
loudspeaker. Tonight, Sinatra and Como had been joined
by Vic Damone, for a triple serving of Italian syrup. Jackie
and Tom lingered over an extra cappucino before getting
in their cars and driving the few blocks to the Irish pub.

"You're going to love this place," Tom told her as they
paused outside the doors. "It's nearly as great as some
places I could show you in San Francisco." He pushed
open the door and they went inside.

Bridget O'Malley's was everything Tom had promised,
with lots of atmosphere, friendly people, a battered old
bandstand under soft golden lights, and Guinness on tap.
The walls were hung with reproductions of old newspapers
from key moments in the history of Ireland, the Procla-
mation of the Republic, and a green and yellow Starry Plow
flag. You could always tell the politics of an Irish bar by
what they put on their walls, Jackie noted. This one was a
bit left of center, but not as far left as some she'd been to
in her younger days.

The music hadn't started yet when they arrived, and they
found a couple of seats at one of the long wooden tables
near the front of the room, and hung their jackets there to
reserve them. Then they went to the bar and ordered up
two pints.

Jackie could have stayed at the table and let Tom bring
the pints, but there was something magical in the way a
pint of Guinness was poured into the glass and then settled
from a chaotic maelstrom of light brown bubbles into a
perfect picture of black and cream perfection. She preferred
to sit at the bar and watch the process with her own eyes,
especially since it had been so long since she'd done it.

The bartender—a large, powerfully built man with dark,
curly hair—poured the pints expertly, and placed them on
a mat near the taps to settle. He gave Jackie a wink. "This

is the good stuff,'' he said, nodding at the full pint glasses.

"Best in the world," she agreed.

Being here brought her marriage to mind all over again, despite her best intentions not to think of it tonight. Cooper hadn't cared for the bars, the beer, the music, or much of anything else about being Irish that Jackie's parents had taught her to love and appreciate. He had been raised ignorant of his heritage, and preferred to stay that way. It was one of the things Frances had particularly disliked about him, though Jackie supposed you could take that part away and Frances would still have had plenty to dislike.

The mirror at the back of the bar was pasted over with sports headlines from the year Clare had won the all-Ireland Hurling championships. "Let me guess—you're a Clare man," she said to the bartender.

"Ah, you shoulda seen that game," he said, pointing a thumb backwards over his shoulder at the yellowing papers. "The Saffron and Blue came from behind at the last and gave Offaly an arse-whipping like they hadn't had in years."

Jackie *had* seen the game, and she wouldn't exactly call Clare's victory an arse-whipping, but it had been satisfying in the extreme to see an underdog team bring in their first All-Ireland victory in eighty years. Hurling was the most amazing sport, Jackie thought, sort of a cross between Gaelic football and a hockey riot. It made any American sport look gentlemanly and subdued by comparison. She decided she really must get in here one weekend soon and take in a match.

She settled down on her barstool with her chin on her hands and watched her Guinness resolve itself in the pint glass and smiled contentedly. "This is a good place," she said to Tom.

"Told you so," he said, tossing a bag of vinegar crisps onto the bar in front of her. "You should learn to listen to me." He glanced at his watch. "It's not quite eight—we've still got lots of time before we have to pick up the kids at midnight,'' he told her.

"They'll be hyper from chocolate and sodas," Jackie guessed, "and they'll have to tell us the plots of all three movies, and neither of them will want to sleep until about four A.M."

"And they'll be horsing around and pretending to kick and punch one another, and they'll both quote lines from Bruce Lee movies all the way home," Tom added.

" 'O'Hara's treachery has disgraced us!' " Jackie quoted.

They looked at one another and shook their heads.

"I think we made a mistake," Jackie said.

"Big mistake," Tom agreed.

They both laughed. Jackie found herself enjoying immensely the degree of comfort she felt. Dating was a dismal activity in her book, and first dates were sort of a personal Hell of hers, but this one was proving to be a pleasant exception.

They sat and talked and nursed their pints until the band began to play, agreeing on the best traditional band—Altán, the best whiskey—Tullamore Dew, and the greatest hero of Irish history—Michael Collins. They both liked Guinness, and Caffrey's Ale, and Tyrone crystal, and Taytos, the delicious potato crisps.

They both hated cutesy pseudo-Irishness, all St. Patrick's day hype—especially green beer—those annoying deodorant soap commercials, and all that tinkly-twinkly 'Celtic New Age' music that most people seemed to think was what Irish music was all about.

"Movies about Ireland?" Jackie inquired.

"Depends," said Tom cautiously.

"*Shake Hands with the Devil*," she tried.

"Revisionist. Hated it."

"*Circle of Friends*?"

"Romantic. Loved it."

The next few hours went by like minutes in a haze of good music and good company. Finally the band started packing up, and Tom looked at his watch. "Time to pick up the kids," he said, with a touch of regret in his voice that Jackie couldn't mistake. Belatedly, Jackie remembered she hadn't yet called Evan Stillman with what she suspected about the burglary of Winnie Swann's house. He'd be home in bed by now, she imagined. She'd call him first thing in the morning.

They got up reluctantly, and said goodnight to the bartender. Tom put an arm over Jackie's shoulders on their way out the door. Her heart jumped nearly out of her chest. How fast did she want this thing to move, anyway? She wished she knew.

They had left Tom's van in front of Guido's, and brought Jackie's Blazer to the bar. Jackie drove them to the Sofia and they parked a short way down the block, close enough to see the kids getting out of the movie, and be seen by them.

"I hope I didn't make you uncomfortable back there," Tom said quietly, after she had turned off the motor and they had waited a few moments in silence.

"No, I don't think uncomfortable is what I would have said," Jackie told him. "It's just that I just got out of a relationship . . ."

"And you're not ready to start anything up right now?" He looked at her steadily, and he seemed ready to accept a gentle rejection, but not especially happy about it.

Jackie shook her head and smiled. "No, I don't think I would have said that, either, exactly," she said, very softly.

Tom put a hand on her neck and drew her gently toward him across the gap between the car seats. Jackie felt dizzy and more than a little afraid. There was a loud noise from outside the car, and Jackie nearly jumped out of her skin. Across the street, the doors of the theater had flown outward with a bang, and dozens, then hundreds of teenagers

and adults poured out onto the sidewalk in front of the
Sofia.

Tom laughed. "Hold that thought," he told her. "Guess
we'd better go collect the next generation."

"Right." Jackie swallowed hard. That had been close.
Too close? Maybe not. Maybe that was the problem.

They climbed down from the Blazer and walked across
the street to the brightly lit theater, where they waited while
throngs of ardent martial arts moviegoers continued to
stream out, seemingly more than the old movie palace could
possibly hold. Still no sign of Peter and Grania.

Jackie caught sight of Peter's best friend, Isaac Cook,
coming out of the far doors with a couple of companions.
"Isaac!" she called.

"Oh, hi, Ms. Walsh," said Isaac, walking over to her.
"What are you doing here?"

"Didn't you see Peter inside, with Grania? He said they
were going to meet you here."

"Oh, they were here, all right," said Isaac. "Some old
guy picked them up about half an hour ago. He said it was
some kind of family emergency. It was just before the end
of *Game of Death*, too. Man, they missed it. It was awe-
some! Is everything all right?"

Jackie and Tom looked at one another, fear dawning on
both their faces. "No, it's not," said Jackie. "What did
this man look like?"

"Really old. About a hundred. Walked with a cane. You
mean you don't know? You didn't send him?"

"No, Isaac. I didn't send anyone."

"We're calling the police," said Tom, his voice shaking.

"My house is only a few blocks from here," Jackie said.
"We can call from there."

Jackie pulled up in front of the townhouse with a screech
of brakes and parked halfway up on the sidewalk in her
haste. The phone was ringing when they got to the door.

Jake was barking from the back yard, where Jackie had left him earlier.

Jackie fumbled with the key, finally getting it into the lock and nearly stumbling inside in her eagerness to reach the phone before it stopped ringing. She slammed her leg into a table on her way across the room and reached the phone, gasping with pain.

"Hello?" she croaked, stabbing the speaker button. A raspy voice rang out in the quiet of the living room. "Bring the money and whatever else you may have found, and meet me at the intersection of Plains Parkway and the Old Springfield Road in half an hour. Northeast corner."

"Where are Peter and Grania?"

"I have them nearby," the man said, and there was something terribly familiar about that voice. "No police! If you involve the police, I'll kill them."

"Judge Hockersmith? Is that you? You harm a hair on my son and I swear I'll . . ."

The phone went dead.

Jackie turned to look at Tom, who was still standing in the open doorway, shock and confusion mingling on his features.

"We're not calling the police," Jackie told him. "You heard what he said."

"What is this all about?" Tom asked. "Who the hell is Judge Hockersmith, and why has he got our kids? What's all this about money? Jackie, what the hell is going on here?"

CHAPTER 23

"I'll explain on the way, I promise. Plains Parkway. Old Springfield Road. Northeast corner," Jackie repeated to herself as she ran up the stairway and down the hall to her bedroom. Tom was right behind her. "Explain now. Please," he pleaded. "What's this all about? What money?"

Jackie dropped to her knees and dug into the back of her bedroom closet, where the bundles of outdated bills she had taken from Winnie's living room wall were stuffed into an old suitcase. She pulled the suitcase out and opened it. The bundles of bills filled the suitcase, and a few tumbled out onto the floor.

"This money." She realized suddenly that she'd never counted the money and had no idea how much was left of the original amount. She supposed it didn't matter at this point.

Tom knelt down by the suitcase and picked up one of the bills from a loose bundle. He looked at it closely, and turned it over in his hand. "This isn't even real money," he said, obviously confused.

"I said I'd explain on the way," said Jackie. "Now carry this to my car. I'll get Jake. We've only just got enough time to get out there." She reached under a magazine on her dresser, snatched up the small white box she had put there the day before, and put it in her shirt pocket. Then she hurried past Tom, who was closing up the suitcase full of money, ran to the back door, and called for Jake.

On the way out of town to the remote area Henry Hockersmith had specified on the telephone, Jackie filled Tom in on Winnie and Franklin and Barney and Lefty, a.k.a. Judge Henry Hockersmith. She explained about the bank robbery that had taken place one summer day seventy years ago, and the men who'd kept it a secret ever since, quietly dividing the income from selling off the money that had become worthless as legal tender practically overnight.

"Franklin was always afraid that Lefty—Judge Hockersmith—would make a move against him. I think he knew all along what a dangerous man he really was. When Henry Hockersmith was shot in the hand and lost his thumb, Franklin kept it. I guess he thought it was his insurance against Henry."

She told him about finding the mummified thumb in the bathroom, and finding Barney Dorfmeier dead only twelve hours ago now, though that seemed like something from another lifetime as they raced down the black ribbon of road in the light of a full moon, on their way to confront the man who had stolen their children.

"So how does this Judge Hockersmith know you've got the money?"

"Because he went looking for it in Franklin's house, and it was gone. I guess I must have skipped that part, but the house was broken into last night, and torn completely apart by someone looking for the money, and probably for the thumb, too."

"Couldn't that have been the other guy—what was his name? Barney?"

"If you believe his granddaughter, Barney Dorfmeier was in Cleveland until the next morning. His health was a lot more delicate than Henry's, too, and I have no reason to believe that he was Franklin's enemy—quite the opposite, in fact. Henry Hockersmith, on the other hand, is a whole different story.''

''So you'd removed the money when you found it in the wall?'' Tom asked.

''Not right then, but the next time we went back. Franklin's son from a previous marriage showed up and claimed ownership of the house. He allowed us to remove Winnie's possessions from the house, and we just sort of included the money in that general category.''

''I see. Go on.''

''We patched up the hole we took the money from, but it would have been pretty easy to see where we did it, and that the patch job was fresh. Judge Hockersmith had seen us at the house once before, and Dwight obligingly told him that we were friends of Winnie's, and that I was a detective.''

''You're a detective?''

''No, I'm not. A lot of people seem to think I am, but that's a whole different story.'' Jackie hoped there'd be time to tell the whole story later, when they had rescued their children.

''From there I guess it wasn't such a far-flung speculation on Henry's part that I might have the money, or know where it was, at least.''

''How did they know where to find the kids?''

''It had to be Angela. I ran into her this afternoon in town. At least I thought I was just running into her. She could very easily have followed me there from home.''

''Jackie, I'm sorry if I seem to be having trouble following all this,'' said Tom, glancing anxiously out the car window as though he might actually be able to tell how near their destination they were. ''You have to admit it's a lot to absorb all at once.''

''Oh God, Tom, I'm sorry you're having to find out everything this way,'' said Jackie, ''but it's not the sort of

thing you usually discuss on a first date. I would have gotten around to telling you sooner or later. I swear I had no
idea there was any danger to the kids.'' She risked a look
across the car at Tom's face. His expression was anxious,
fearful, but not angry, at least as far as she could tell.

There was a long silence. Finally, he said, ''It's not your
fault. We just have to get them back—that's the only important thing.'' He reached around to the back seat and
patted Jake. ''And that's what you're going to do for us,
isn't it, boy?'' Jake whined anxiously. Jackie knew he had
no real idea what was going on, but he could sense the
tension in the air, and smell their fear, and he was on the
alert for anything.

Peter's red sweatshirt was still in the back of the Blazer,
and Jake had already proved how accomplished he was at
tracking. ''If we can get close enough to where they are to
pick up a trail,'' Tom said, ''I know Jake can find them.''

''I know he can, too,'' said Jackie, trying to keep her
voice steady as she sped the car along the highway toward
the rendezvous point.

Tom reached out a hand and put it over hers as it rested
on the gear shift. ''We'll get them back,'' he told her.
''That's a promise.''

The highway was straight and almost deserted this time
of night. Jackie saw only a few cars behind her, and fewer
ahead as she sped through the night to the place Henry
Hockersmith had specified, glancing anxiously at the clock
on the dashboard every minute or so, fearful of what might
happen if she arrived late. If anything happened to those
kids, she'd never be able to forgive herself, she knew.

She should have taken the time to call Evan when she
got home this afternoon, before she and Peter went to meet
Tom and Grania. Or she should have called him when she
stopped off to leave Jake in the back yard before she and
Tom went out to dinner in the evening. If only she'd done
that!

If, Jackie reminded herself, was an awfully large word. *If* Evan had believed a word she said anyway; *if* he thought that there was any believable connection between the seventy-year-old bank robbery and the burglary of Winnie Swann's house; *if* he'd been willing to arrest a prominent citizen of Palmer, a former judge, the father of a City Councilman, then none of this might have happened.

If, if, if. Those things probably wouldn't have happened anyway, Jackie told herself, but it didn't do any good.

"How close are we to the intersection?" Tom asked her.

"A couple of miles, I think."

"Drop me off just before you get there, but out of sight of the intersection," Tom said. "Jake and I are going hunting."

Jackie slowed down as she began to recognize landmarks that told her she was approaching the intersection of Old Springfield Road and the Plains Parkway. The area between here and Palmer had grown up a lot over the years, and this place was no longer as far out from the city as it had been when she was a child. It was hard to know exactly where she was.

She stopped just before the road curved sharply, switching off her headlights to avoid alerting anyone who might be watching for them near the intersection. She looked up at the rearview mirror. A pair of headlights was visible in the distance. As she watched, the car went past and kept on going.

Tom got out and opened the back door. Jake whined again, waiting for a clue as to what was going on, and what his part in it might be. His big, black ears stood up straight, and he sniffed the air as if it might hold the information he needed.

"Do you want to take a flashlight?" Jackie asked.

"Better not advertise we're out there," said Tom. He looked up at the moon, high overhead now, like the sun at noon. "I think we'll have enough light. I wish the wind hadn't come up so hard though.'' The gentle breezes of earlier in the day had grown into a cool, brisk wind. Jackie realized it was going to make Jake's job quite a bit harder.

"Hey, Jake and I can handle it," Tom told her. "It may take us a little longer, that's all."

He knelt down and put his arms around the big shepherd's neck. "It's up to you now, Jake. We're counting on you." He snapped the leather lead onto Jake's collar.

Jackie reached into the back seat and handed Tom the red sweatshirt. He took it, holding onto her hand for a long moment, then squeezing it hard just before he let go, taking the sweatshirt with him. "We're going to cover a radius around the intersection and see what Jake can sniff up," he said. "Don't worry about where we are—we'll find you."

"Please be careful," Jackie said.

"You, too," he said. He paused, looking at her, as though he might be about to say more. His eyes dropped away from hers. "Be careful."

The man and the dog walked quietly into the moonlit trees. A few seconds later they were swallowed up as though they never existed. Jackie felt a chill of fear and aloneness that nearly took her breath away.

She put the car in reverse and pulled it around to face the highway again. Carefully, she pulled out onto the road, not wanting noise or a dust cloud to provide a clue that she hadn't come straight from the highway. When she was completely off the side of the road, she turned her headlights back on and began looking for the sign that would tell her she had reached her destination.

She saw the road sign less than half a mile from where she'd dropped off Tom and Jake. There were no cars in evidence, but she pulled up to the northeast corner where the land started to rise to a wooded hill, parked under some trees, and turned off the car's engine. She got out of the Blazer and opened the back door to get the suitcase.

"Don't make any sudden moves," said a voice behind her. "I've got a gun."

CHAPTER 24

It was Henry Hockersmith, sounding nervous but determined. There was no reason not to believe him, Jackie decided, and several good reasons not to get herself shot. She pulled the suitcase full of money from the back seat slowly and carefully, turning around and setting it down on the ground in front of her.

Henry Hockersmith pointed a gun at her with his left hand. His right hand was in his coat pocket, and his eagle-headed cane was hooked over the crook of his right arm.

"It's all in here," she said, pointing to the suitcase. There didn't seem to be any point in telling him about the real money she'd found hidden in the hole with the obsolete bills. She'd forgotten to include it in her haste to meet him, and he almost certainly knew nothing about it anyway. Henry stared greedily at the suitcase. "Push it over here with your foot. Slowly, now," he instructed.

"Where's my son and his friend?" Jackie demanded.

"They're perfectly safe, a little way from here," said Henry, hooking one foot over the suitcase and pulling it closer to him. "If I get what I came here for, they'll be released unharmed."

"Unharmed like Barney Dorfmeier? That was a nice lit-

tle surprise you left for us at Mrs. Batcheler's house today.''

''Barney was a pitiful weakling, even when he was
twenty-one,'' said the Judge with a derisive snort. ''He
hadn't grown any backbone in the past seventy years, either. As soon as he found out you knew what we'd done,
he'd have spilled his guts to you. Anyway, I didn't do anything his own body wouldn't have done to him on its own
in pretty short order.''

''So that takes care of Barney. Who was Franklin going
to tell?''

Henry shook his head. ''Franklin was the strongest and
smartest of the three of us,'' he said, admiration plain in
his voice. ''He'd never have breathed a word to anyone—
not deliberately. The whole thing was his idea, originally.''

''The bank robbery? That was Franklin's idea? I don't
believe you.''

The Judge gestured, and the gun wavered a bit. ''Oh, it
was just something we dreamed up late one night when we
were all roaring drunk, our last year in college. We'd probably have forgotten about it by the time the hangovers were
gone, but Franklin kept thinking about it, planning it. It
was just sort of an intellectual exercise to him at first, I'll
admit.''

''When did it become more than intellectual?'' Jackie
asked him. It might be a good idea to keep the judge talking
while she figured out as much as she could about the situation she was in. Right now it didn't look good, but she
could always hope some opportunity would present itself.

''Franklin showed me the plan he'd worked up,'' said
Henry. ''He was proud of it, and it really was an amazing
piece of work. Franklin had a mind for detail the likes of
which most people only dream about. He worked it all up,
and said it was a shame he couldn't use it for a term paper,
after all the hours he'd put into it. Then he threw it into a
wastepaper basket.''

"But you took it out again."

"You have no idea what a brilliant plan it was," Henry insisted. "He'd worked out every detail, studied the layout of the bank, and the schedule of the armored cars that transferred money, and the shifts of the guards, and dozens of things I can't remember after all these years. And it was all just for fun! He'd have thrown it away and never given it another thought except to laugh about it once in a while."

"But not you," Jackie said. "You couldn't let it go at that, could you?"

"Of course I couldn't," the Judge replied. "So I made a study of Franklin's plan and set about convincing him— not that it would work, because he knew that already—but that we should actually go ahead and do it."

"Where did Barney Dorfmeier come in?"

"We needed a third man to drive the car," said Henry. "Barney would have been my last choice on earth, but he was devoted to Franklin—followed him everywhere like some sort of a puppy dog. When he found out we were discussing the adventure of a lifetime, he begged to be included. Oh, Franklin wouldn't hear of it at first, but Barney wouldn't leave him alone about it. Finally, he gave in and allowed him to drive the car. Of course this was only after I'd succeeded in convincing Franklin to go through with the robbery in the first place. That took the better part of six months all by itself."

"So you robbed the bank, but before you could get away, you were shot in the hand by a bank guard," Jackie prompted.

"I see you've been doing your homework," said Henry, nodding in satisfaction. He was beginning to enjoy his starring role in this movie of his memories. "Franklin wanted to get me to a hospital, then turn ourselves in. I had to threaten to shoot him left-handed to get him to change his mind.

"I would probably have died from loss of blood, but

Franklin knew a lot about first aid, and he slowed down the bleeding while we were driving away, and then treated me for shock while we were hiding out.''

"Where did you hide out, anyway?''

"There's a cabin not far from here,'' said Henry, indicating the direction with a nod of his head over his shoulder. "A lodge, actually. It belonged to my parents, but they were away in Europe at the time, and I had the run of the place. That's where we went, after we ditched the car.''

He took his ruined hand out of his pocket and looked at it. "My thumb was hanging by a bit of flesh. Franklin cut it off. Then he stitched up the hand himself with silk thread from my mother's sewing cabinet.'' He laughed bitterly. "Maybe Franklin should've been a seamstress instead of an accountant. He did a hell of a neat job.''

"But how did you cover up what had happened to your hand? Didn't you have to go back to school?''

"That was part of the beauty of the timing,'' said the Judge. "The school term had let out, and the three of us had graduated with our bachelor's degrees. We made up a story about getting my hand caught in a boat motor to cover with my parents when they came back at the end of the summer. They never questioned it.''

"So how did you end up getting stuck with the money?'' Jackie asked.

"We agreed to hide the money and not spend any of it for at least one year,'' said Henry. "That was to make sure the heat had died down over the robbery—Franklin's idea, again. At the end of that time we were going to divide it up and leave the country. In those days a lot of Latin American countries didn't have extradition treaties with the United States. I didn't plan to go to law school, you know—I planned to spend the rest of my days on some tropical beach, living the life of Riley. But life had other plans for me. For all of us.'' There was no mistaking the bitterness and regret that crept into his voice as he remembered his youthful dreams, and how badly they had gone wrong.

"Franklin was to be responsible for hiding the money, and for dividing it up at the end of the year," Henry continued, "since neither Barney nor I doubted his honesty or his competence. It was also Franklin's idea that neither of us were to know where the money was hidden, in case one of us was arrested."

"But before you could divide the money, it became worthless," said Jackie.

"Yes," said Henry, his distress at this turn of events still evident even after all these years. "The currency was called back, and suddenly we were the owners of one hundred and fifty thousand dollars in worthless bills."

"Until Franklin discovered he could sell them off for their value to collectors."

"Yes, but it was many years before that value amounted to much. Once it became worth his while, Franklin traveled out of town to sell off a small number of bills twice a year, and divided up the proceeds among the three of us. He and Barney remained friends, but I distanced myself from both of them and pursued a career in Law at Northwestern. Many years later, I came back to Palmer and established a practice here."

"Franklin was afraid of you. Why was that?"

"After many years had gone by, and I had married Dwight's mother and established myself on the bench, I began to worry about what would happen if Franklin were to slip up and somehow implicate me in the robbery. His mind wasn't nearly devious enough to be safe from such an eventuality."

"Not like yours, you mean."

"That's exactly what I mean," the Judge said, not at all apologetic for his natural deviousness but seeming rather proud of it for its practical value. "I had a career to look out for—a standing in the community. I had to make sure

Franklin understood just how far I was willing to go to protect myself.''

"And that's when he told you he still had your thumb," Jackie guessed.

"He'd kept it just in case I ever decided to threaten him. I'd underestimated Franklin, it seems."

"He knew you well," Jackie commented.

"Better than I knew him. I couldn't see it at the time, but I know now that our secret was safe with Franklin."

"Then why did you kill him?" Jackie asked.

"Kill him?" The Judge sounded astonished. "No one killed Franklin Swann—he fell off a ladder and broke his neck!"

"I think someone may have helped him fall off that ladder," said Jackie.

"You think too much for your own good," Henry snorted. "Now step over here, bend down very slowly and open this suitcase."

Jackie did as she was told, bending over carefully, never taking her eyes off Henry Hockersmith. She watched the barrel of his gun following her down, and the glint of his eyes in the moonlight.

Was she going to get out of this alive? Was anyone? Why would Henry let the kids go, or her either, at this point? Although he claimed to be innocent of Franklin's death, he'd already confessed to killing Barney Dorfmeier for fear he'd talk. Surely he wouldn't have said that to someone who could walk away and tell everything to the police.

It was more than the money he wanted, Jackie realized—he wanted everyone who knew about his crime wiped from off the face of the earth. It couldn't matter that much for him alone at this point, but it was important to protect his son's political career.

Everyone, she realized, meant her and Frances and Winnie, and anyone else who got in his way, like Tom and

Grania and Peter. His only choice, the way he doubtless saw the situation, was to kill them all.

She stepped away from the suitcase, and Henry knelt down before it, cradling his cane in the crook of his right arm, and fingering the bundles of bills with the remaining fingers of that hand while the left hand continued to point the gun at her.

She knew his concentration was divided, and thought briefly about what she might be able to do about it, but he was standing so close. The open lid of the suitcase was between her and any opportunity to kick him, and she wasn't absolutely certain he wouldn't be able to get off a shot in her direction if she tried something now. As inaccurate as a pistol could be, she thought, from that range it wouldn't be all that hard to hit her.

All she could do, Jackie decided, was wait for her chance, but if a good chance didn't come along she was willing to risk a bad one. What she wasn't willing to do was let herself be led meekly to her own slaughter, or to let any harm come to her son.

Henry felt around the bottom and sides of the suitcase, moving the money aside and searching for something else that he wasn't finding. "Where is it?" he asked, his voice growing shrill. He felt through the pockets in the lid of the suitcase. "Are you hiding it? Or didn't you bring it with you?" He looked up at her, a half-crazed desperation in his eyes.

For half a second Jackie wondered if Henry had lost what was left of his marbles. Then she remembered what it was he must be talking about. She reached into her shirt pocket and took out the small white box. "Could this be what you're looking for?" she asked. She opened the box and lifted out its awful contents, holding the dried, blackened thumb out in front of Henry's face.

He got up, leaning heavily on the cane, which almost went out from under him on the uneven ground. He righted himself, grunting with the effort. "Give it to me," he said, panting.

"Here you go, Henry," said Jackie, and threw the thumb as hard as she could.

CHAPTER 25

The Judge watched helplessly as the mummified thumb sailed over his head. He gasped, eyes wide, as it disappeared from sight and only a slight rustle in the darkness betrayed it as it landed behind him, several feet away. "Damn you!" he screamed at Jackie, then turned toward where his thumb had gone, almost falling again in his haste, and saving himself at the last moment with his walking stick.

As soon as he turned his back, Jackie threw herself at his legs and brought him to the ground before he could take two steps. He squealed with pain, and she didn't feel so much as a twinge of sympathy. She heard the gun hit the ground a few feet beyond them, knocked from his hand as she fell. She could see the moonlight glinting off the polished metal.

She put one foot in Henry's back and launched herself in the direction of the gun, but her other foot got tangled up with his right arm and the cane, and she went flying into the dirt, still a couple of feet short of her objective, and shy one shoe in the scuffle.

Jackie heard the sound of someone descending the hill above them in a hurry. Tom? He wouldn't know about the gun—she had to get it before the Judge could. She twisted herself around and jerked the cane out from between her feet, tossed it aside, then attempted to get up again.

Two clawlike hands gripped her around both ankles and held on with a strength that surprised her. She kicked once, losing her other shoe, but the hands held on. Someone burst into the clearing.

"Dad? Are you all right?" Dwight Hockersmith's voice was shaking with fear.

"Get the gun, you idiot!" the old man shouted at his son.

"Gun?"

"Over there!" Henry had to release one of Jackie's ankles to point out the gun lying just out of Jackie's reach, barely visible in the pale light through the trees. She took advantage of the moment to deliver a barefooted kick to his head, but at the last instant she pulled back for fear of breaking his neck. He yelped anyway as her foot connected with his skull, and she managed to drag them a little closer to the gun.

Dwight dropped to his hands and knees near her head, looking for the gun in the pale moonlight. Luckily, his own shadow was obscuring it from him for the moment, but Jackie knew exactly where it was. She pulled at her captive foot and kicked Henry again, but to no avail. His fingers dug into her leg like steel.

Suddenly she remembered something. Her arm stretched out and she scrambled outwards in the dirt with her hands, as far as she could reach. Just as Dwight caught sight of the gun and bent down to retrieve it, her fingers found the discarded walking stick. She grasped the wooden shaft and brought the metal end down on the back of Dwight's head with a sharp, wet whack. He cried out once, and collapsed onto the ground.

She kicked backwards again immediately, this time not sparing the old man all the force she could put into the blow. He let go with a shriek of pain and Jackie was up and running for the gun. She grabbed it and turned around, dropping the cane to the ground. Henry was lying on his stomach, his good hand wiping dirt from his eyes, spitting and cursing. Dwight was moaning, but he was conscious.

"Both of you get up," said Jackie, backing away from Dwight's reach, Henry's gun held firmly in both hands. "You're taking me to Peter."

Dwight raised himself to his feet slowly, and brought a hand up to the back of his head, then brought it back to his face, covered in blood. He looked as though he might faint. "I'm bleeding!" he protested.

"It's a scalp wound," Jackie told him. "There's always a lot of blood with a scalp wound." She looked around her quickly for her shoes.

"But I might bleed to death!"

Old Judge Hockersmith pulled himself up onto his hands and knees, not without difficulty. "Oh, shut up, Dwight, before I put a tourniquet around your neck," he snapped at his son. He tried to get up onto his feet, but seemed to lack the strength. "I need my cane," he said to Jackie. "I don't think I'm going to be able to get to my feet without it."

"You figure out a way," she told him. "I'll wait." An old dog might learn new tricks, Jackie thought, but it didn't make him a different dog. Franklin had known Henry couldn't be trusted seventy years ago when he decided to keep the thumb—Jackie wasn't going to doubt that wisdom now.

Snarling, the Judge crawled slowly along the ground for a few feet, running his hands back and forth over the surface. He grasped a handful of dirt and leaves, inspected it, and cast it aside.

"What on earth are you doing now?" Jackie demanded.

"My thumb," he moaned. "I have to find my thumb!"

"Oh, for pity's sake!" Jackie snapped. "You've gone the past seventy years without it—who cares if you have it now?'' Her nerves were showing. She took a deep breath and tried to calm herself as much as possible under the circumstances.

"I care!" wailed Henry. "It's part of me! Franklin hid it away, and now you've thrown it away, and I want the damned thing back!"

Jackie could see she was going to have no end of trouble with Henry Hockersmith if she didn't reunite him with his missing thumb. "Just stay where you are," she instructed him. "You too, Dwight. Don't either of you move."

She faced in the direction she'd been looking in when she threw the thumb and calculated the area where it probably would have landed. Keeping the gun pointing at the two men, she walked in the direction of her throw, scanning the ground at intervals, and managing to find both her shoes in the process. The thumb was light and she wasn't terribly strong, so it probably wouldn't have traveled far.

Finally, after several false alarms with twigs, she spotted it, black and awful in the moonlight. Grimacing, she picked it up. "Okay, I've got it. Henry, you can get up now."

Henry crawled over to the nearest tree and pulled himself up by supporting himself against the trunk. "Can I have my cane back, now?"

"I'm afraid not. It'll be slower going without it, but I'm damned if I'm going to provide you with a weapon. We already know what kind of damage it can do." She pointed toward Dwight, who was still uttering low-pitched cries of pain. "You can have this, though." She stepped closer to him and tossed the thumb, underhanded this time, into his waiting hands.

He tucked it carefully into an inside pocket of his suit coat. "Thank you," he said, barely loud enough for her to hear.

Jackie bent down and closed the suitcase, then picked it up by its handle. She wished she didn't have to carry it, but it didn't seem wise to give it to Dwight—he might get the notion of taking off with it, and Jackie wasn't at all sure, despite her brave talk, that she could actually shoot him. As for Henry, he was going to have a hard enough time walking through the woods without the help of his eagle-headed walking stick.

"Time to get up, Councilman," she informed Dwight. He raised himself to his hands and knees and finally, painfully, to his feet, giving her a look that tried to be menacing, but missed its mark by yards. It was that baby face, she supposed.

"Now we're going to find my son," she told them. "You're going to put your hands on top of your heads and lead me to the cabin, and after all we've been through here tonight, if either of you thinks I won't shoot you if you try anything—anything at all—you'd better keep thinking until you get it right."

"You wouldn't shoot us in the back, would you?" Dwight whimpered.

"I sure as hell wouldn't wait for you to turn around," said Jackie. "Now put your hands on top of your heads and move."

The two men walked through the trees ahead of her, hands clasped on top of their heads, picking their way slowly through the rocks and branches. Several times they had to stop and wait for the Judge to hug a tree and get his breath, or to recover from stumbling.

Jackie picked her way carefully, fearful of tripping over something and losing control of the situation. She was grateful for the light of the moon, but it wasn't enough to make the going easy. After what seemed like hours but was probably only twenty minutes or so, she could see a light ahead, coming from a big house with a screened porch, nestled in a clearing at the top of a small rise.

"That's my family's lodge—the hideout Franklin and Barney and I stayed at after the robbery," said Henry. "The children are in there." They crossed the clearing and the

Judge stopped at the porch steps as though expecting Jackie to go ahead.

"You first," she said, poking him with the gun. She could have enjoyed playing this tough-guy role—sort of a cross between Bogie and Richard Widmark—if there weren't so much as stake. She controlled the shaking that threatened to betray her terror, and hoped to anyone who listened to such requests that she wouldn't make any major mistakes in there.

The Judge climbed wearily up the steps, almost gasping for breath. Dwight walked behind him, blood still trickling down the back of his neck and onto his shirt collar. Jackie brought up the rear.

"I'm going to need to take my hands down to open the door," the Judge informed her as they stepped up onto the porch.

"Slowly," Jackie warned.

Quivering with fatigue but still too proud to complain, the old man brought his hands down from his head and fumbled with the knob. The door opened and he stepped into the doorway, followed by Dwight and Jackie. "She's got a gun!" he said to someone in the room as he stepped inside.

"That's all right," said Angela Hockersmith. "I've got one, too."

CHAPTER 26

Jackie and Angela stared one another down over the barrels of their respective weapons. Jackie looked Angela in the eye with what she hoped was an expression that conveyed more determination than fear.

Angela returned her stare, but Jackie could sense her apprehension. She'd surely been expecting Jackie to come back as Henry's prisoner, or perhaps not to come back at all, and certainly not with a gun in her husband's back. This probably wasn't at all how she'd been expecting things to turn out.

Jackie motioned the two men inside the doorway and off to her left so she could get a clear look at the room, a large, high-ceilinged space furnished with deep leather chairs and sofas, and surrounded by a high, railed mezzanine. Rough-wooded tables stood here and there along the walls, holding family photographs and an impressive collection of old porcelain and china.

Peter and Grania were tied to two kitchen chairs, side by side, across the room from Jackie, on a stone hearth in front of a huge, empty fireplace. They sagged with relief when they caught sight of her.

Angela stood close behind them. "Dwight, Dad, thank

God you're back,'' she told Henry. "I was afraid something awful had happened to you.''

"Something awful did happen to us, you idiot!'' Henry snapped at her. "We're being held at gunpoint!''

When Angela had fully absorbed the fact of Jackie pointing a gun at her husband and her father-in-law, she redirected her own gun down in front of her, toward the two teenagers. Jackie's heart dropped into her shoes, but she tried hard not to show it to the kids.

"Mom, I'm sorry,'' said Peter, tears standing in his eyes. "He said he knew you. He said there'd been an accident!''

"We thought it was okay to go with him,'' said Grania, trying hard not to cry. "He said . . .'' Jackie tried to signal her to silence with a look before she could mention her father or ask where he was. Grania seemed to get the message. She choked down the rest of the sentence and sat silently, her head turned away from the sight of the gun barrel so close to her face.

"She wouldn't even be here if she hadn't insisted on coming along with the boy,'' said Henry. "It wasn't her I was after.''

"It's okay, kids,'' said Jackie. "We're getting out of this, don't worry.'' She sincerely hoped she was right—she'd always tried never to break a promise to her son, and this would be a terrible time to start.

Jackie motioned Henry and Dwight to a position on her other side, where she could better see them and Angela at the same time. "Stand close to one another,'' she told them. She didn't want to be worried about which of them to cover if push came to shove, and it certainly looked as though it might.

"Can I put my hands down too, at least?'' Dwight whined. "My arms are killing me!''

"Very slowly,'' said Jackie. "Don't scare me, whatever you do, or I'll probably shoot you before I have time to think about it.''

As Dwight put his arms down and walked over to stand by his father, Angela noticed the blood on his hands and head. "Oh, my poor baby!" she squealed. Dwight was pale-faced and still swaying a bit, fresh blood running down into his shirt collar, which was already stained reddish-black with the blood that had dried while they walked from the meeting place in the woods to the cabin.

"It's all right, darling," Dwight croaked, but his wife's concern only seemed to weaken him more. He groaned and leaned on Henry for support.

"Stand on your own two feet, you moron!" Henry protested, shaking off Dwight's arm. "Am I the only person in this family with any guts?" He gave his son a look of pure disgust.

"What did she do to you?" Angela asked Dwight, still managing to hold the gun on Peter and Grania while she turned her head this way and that, trying to get a look at Dwight's wound. "If anything happens to my husband I'll kill you!" she promised Jackie.

"She hit me over the head with a tree branch or something," Dwight moaned, sounding surprised and injured. "And she hurt Dad, too."

Angela looked at Henry's face, which was dirty and scuffed and bleeding slightly here and there, then seemed to decide she was more worried about Dwight. "Come here, sweetheart," she said to him, "and let me look at that. You might need stitches."

"Forget it," Jackie told Dwight before he could complete a step. "You stay right where you are, or it's going to take a lot more than a few stitches to fix what I'm going to do to you."

She turned back to Angela. "You can have your precious husband back as soon as you untie my son and his friend, and let them leave the cabin."

Angela looked for a brief instant as though she might be considering Jackie's offer.

"Don't you dare let them go!" barked Henry. "You agreed to this, and you're sticking to it! You agreed to everything we discussed."

Angela looked back and forth between Jackie and Dwight and Henry, anxious and afraid, but she didn't lower the gun. The polished and perfect Mrs. Hockersmith was a little new at this holding-at-gunpoint game, Jackie figured, but then so was she. It was all a little unreal—like starring in a movie whose ending you couldn't remember. There was a long moment of utter silence as they stood on opposite sides of the spacious cabin living room and watched one another. The situation had become a standoff.

Jackie hoped Tom and Jake would arrive soon, but she wasn't sure if that would save the day, or if the kids might end up getting shot anyway. A tight knot of fear wrapped itself around her insides and squeezed.

She looked at Angela, a little less than poised and perfect now, holding a gun on the two trussed-up teenagers, but betraying her nervousness with her body language: shallow breathing and wide, fearful eyes. Maybe this was the weak link she should be exploiting.

"Why should you listen to him?" Jackie asked her, taking the offensive as best she could. "He'll do anything to protect Dwight, but where do you fit in to all this? Can you really trust him not to turn on you? He's already killed one man today because he knew his little secret."

Angela and Dwight both turned to look at Henry, mouths open and eyes bulging in shocked surprise. "Dad?" they chorused.

"Oh, for God's sake," said the old Judge. "I should have known she'd bring that up." He gave Jackie a look that would wilt lettuce.

Jackie shrugged. The old crook had murdered his ex-college roommate this morning. Her only crime was to report that fact. What did he want from her—an apology?

"Dad?" Dwight looked even paler, if possible. "You killed someone? Who?"

"A ninety-one-year-old man named Barney Dorfmeier," Jackie supplied. "I don't know how he managed it, but he already confessed it to me."

"Oh, I'll be glad to tell you how I managed it," said Henry, an unmistakable note of pride in a job well done creeping into his voice. "Barney was taking some very strong medication to lower his blood pressure. His doctor made him write down in a little notebook every time he took one, so he didn't forget and take two. He was getting a little forgetful, and the doctor warned him if he took two pills too close together, his heart might stop altogether."

"How did you get him to take that extra pill?" Jackie asked.

"We were playing checkers up in his room when his granddaughter came in to say you were on your way over," said Henry. "After he took a pill and wrote it down on a page in the notebook, I just waited until he got up to go to the bathroom, and tore out that page. A few minutes later I reminded him that he hadn't taken his pill. He was pretty sure he had, but when he looked in the little notebook there was no note for that day and time."

"So he obligingly took another one."

Henry nodded.

"And then he obligingly died," said Jackie. She sneaked a look at Dwight and Angela, hoping they would be sufficiently dismayed at the notion to turn against the old man.

Dwight looked sick. "Dad, you promised no one would be hurt."

"Oh, grow up, Dwight," snapped Judge Hockersmith. "I promised no such thing. You're the one who kept insisting on that little feature, and I let you convince yourself that's the way it would be, but somewhere in that feeble mind of yours you had to know it wasn't true."

"He's right, Dwight," said Jackie. "Grow up. Your father's been running things his way up until now, but you're a big boy now. Listen to your father and stand on your own two feet for once.''

Dwight looked as though his two feet wouldn't hold him up much longer. Angela looked as though she were wrestling with indecision, but she hadn't yet stopped pointing her gun at the kids. Henry looked at Jackie with venom in his eyes. ''Don't listen to her!'' he ordered his son and daughter-in-law.

''You two didn't know about Barney Dorfmeier,'' Jackie went on, ''so you're not accomplices unless you go on co-operating with Henry from here. If you do that, there's no hope for any of you.''

''The only hope you've got is to stick with me,'' said Henry. ''We get rid of the three of them, bury them where no one will ever find them, and go back home like nothing happened.''

''You got lucky once, Henry,'' Jackie told him. ''You pulled off a bank job and walked away from it free and clear. Don't bet on it happening again, especially if you murder three innocent people.''

She turned her head toward Angela. ''All you have to do is put down that gun right now. Then we'll call the police, and you can have this all behind you.''

''Angela, if you put down that gun, I'll kill you with my bare hands!'' the Judge shouted. ''We've worked for years to get Dwight this close to the mayorship. Think of it! In four years he could be running for Congress, and in eight years you could be redecorating the Governor's mansion!''

Angela seemed to take him at his word. Her hands shook just a bit, but the thought of picking out new drapes as Mrs. Governor Hockersmith seemed a strengthening one, and the gun didn't budge. She looked away from Jackie and steadied herself with a deep breath.

Dwight shook his head. ''I don't think a mayoral campaign is worth someone getting killed,'' he said. ''I don't think even the governership is worth that.'' He sounded a little less convinced about that last idea, Jackie thought.

"Well, what did you think we were doing here?" his father asked him, clearly amazed at his naïveté. "Did you suppose we were going to get the evidence and then leave people who knew about it wandering around town?"

"I didn't want any bloodshed," said Dwight. "I certainly didn't want any murders on my conscience. I just wanted to avoid the scandal of having everyone find out about your past. I guess I just didn't think it through."

"Well, you're thinking now," said Jackie. "I know it must be an unfamiliar sensation, but keep it up a little longer. There are going to be three murders on your conscience. Is that what you want?"

"Take it from me, Dwight, it doesn't matter what's on your conscience as long as you're not in prison," Henry argued. "Do you fancy twenty years behind bars? How well do you think you'd survive that? How well do you think your precious little wife would survive?" He pointed to Angela, whose hair was still impeccable, but whose lip was beginning to tremble.

The front door flew open. For a fraction of a second, Jackie let herself believe that it was Tom and Jake, and that all this would be over in a few seconds. Then she turned her head to look at the doorway.

No such luck.

There was the unmistakably businesslike click of the hammer of a revolver being drawn back. "I want my money, and I want it right now," said Dalton Swann.

CHAPTER 27

Dalton pointed the revolver at each of them in turn. Angela, Dwight, and Henry stared at him in bafflement and disbelief. Jackie's expression was closer to utter exasperation.

"Hand over the money," said Dalton in a dramatic tone straight out of *Public Enemy*. Jackie wanted to tell him that Jimmy Cagney had done it better, but she doubted he'd appreciate the critique.

"Who the hell are you?" Henry demanded. "Do you know this man?" he asked Jackie.

Jackie sighed. "I wish I didn't," she told him, "but then I wish I'd never met any of you."

"I'm Dalton Swann, and you've got one hundred and fifty thousand dollars that belongs to me."

Before Henry could protest that claim, he was startled by a figure even more frightening, looming out of the darkness behind Dalton—his lovely sister, Claire. "What's going on here?" she demanded of her brother, as she squinted at the assembly of gun pointers and pointees, apparently confused. Jackie could scarcely blame her for that.

"*Never mind, Claire!*" he shouted into her ear. "*Go away!* Everybody put down your guns!" Dalton demanded of the rest of them, a bit petulantly.

No one moved except Claire, who, taking her brother's

advice, began to wander around the room, picking up objects and examining them curiously.

"Why aren't you dropping your guns?" Dalton asked. He looked at Jackie, confused.

Jackie looked around the room. Angela eyed Dalton nervously, still keeping her gun pointed at Peter and Grania. Dwight leaned against the nearest wall and held his head in his hands. Henry trembled violently as Claire fingered a celadon vase. Well, concern for his possessions should keep Henry occupied for a few minutes. Now to take care of Dalton, if she could.

"It's like this, Dalton," Jackie explained. "If I don't keep this gun pointed at Dwight and Henry, Angela's going to shoot those two kids tied up in the chairs. If she doesn't keep her gun pointing at the kids, I'm probably going to shoot her in the leg just to get her out of my way."

Angela squirmed, shifting her weight from one threatened leg to another.

"That is I'll shoot her if Henry doesn't kill her with his bare hands, which he just might be able to—he has very strong hands for a man his age." She would probably have bruises, she figured, from his fingers digging into her legs.

"Now if you shoot me," Jackie continued, "Henry's going to make Angela shoot you so you won't take his money." Dalton opened his mouth to protest the ownership of the money, but Jackie stopped him with a wave of her hand. "He thinks it's his money—let's humor him." Dalton closed his mouth again.

"And of course if you shoot Angela, I'm going to shoot you because I don't like you very much." Jackie could tell she was getting cranky under all this stress, but she really didn't care—the time for good manners had passed when Henry had kidnapped the kids and started this whole mess.

"On the other hand," Jackie went on, "you don't really care if Angela shoots my son and his friend, do you?"

Dalton didn't answer, intent on keeping his facts straight

while simultaneously keeping everyone in the room men-
aced by his gun, but Angela immediately saw the logic in
this, and turned her weapon away from Peter and Grania
and toward Dalton.

Jackie stifled a sigh of relief. So far, so good. "And I'm
sure it doesn't matter to you one way or another if I shoot
Dwight and Henry, does it?"

Dalton looked at Jackie intently and blinked twice. He
seemed to be trying to figure out if this was a trick question.

"I mean, think about it—it would save you the trouble,
wouldn't it?"

Dalton nodded.

"But then Angela might get all distraught and fire her
gun, and it's aimed at you."

He nodded again, but looked distinctly uncomfortable.

"I know it's confusing, Dalton, but try to stick with me,
all right? Dwight, Henry, walk—slowly—over there and
sit down on the floor." She pointed to a neutral corner
where she could watch them, but far enough from Peter
and Grania to keep them safe from accidental gunfire if she
had to shoot. "Sit on your hands," she instructed them. If
they got any ideas about taking advantage of the confusion,
she wanted to give herself the edge.

Dwight and Henry put their hands underneath them, but
Henry muttered something under his breath. "Would you
like to share that with the rest of the class, Henry?" Jackie
asked.

He glowered at her.

"That's better," said Jackie. "Okay, Dalton, keep an eye
on those two if you want to walk out of here with your
money."

Dalton turned his gun on Dwight and Henry, but looked
uncertain of the wisdom of it.

"Now I think we've got this straightened out except for
me and you," Jackie said to Dalton, "and I know you don't
care if someone shoots me, but there's someone who might

matter to you a little more," and she turned her sights on Claire. Dalton pointed his gun at Jackie in turn.

"Not perfect, but it works for me," said Jackie. Then something that had been bothering her since Dalton had shown up made its way to her forebrain. "And how in hell did you get here, and how did you find out about the money in the first place?"

"Someone destroyed my house looking for something," said Dalton. "I figured it had to be something valuable. The only person I could think of who'd know what that might be was Winnie."

"Winnie told you about the money?" Jackie couldn't conceal her disbelief.

"I'm sure she wouldn't have if she'd known what she was doing," Dalton allowed. "I got there when she was just waking up from a nap, and she was sort of confused. She thought I was my father."

Jackie looked at Dalton and tried to see the resemblance. It was there in the shape of his face and the general cast of his features, but his personality had put an entirely different stamp on those features, replacing his father's gentleness and good humor with a repellent, mean-spirited aspect. "I'll bet she didn't stay confused for long," she commented.

"Long enough to tell us you'd found the money," said Dalton. "Then Claire and I drove to your house and parked across the street and waited for you to come home. You ran in and left the door open, so I hid outside the door and listened to you talking to someone on the phone."

"That was me," Henry volunteered.

"He mentioned the money," said Dalton, nodding in Henry's direction. "That's when I knew you really had it, and this wasn't all some fantasy of Winnie's."

"Your father may have been forced to leave you the house," said Jackie, "but he didn't leave you that money. The money belongs to Winnie."

"It's going to cost me a small fortune to repair the damage to my house," Dalton said. "I think I'm owed something for that."

"Take it up with Henry over there," said Jackie. "And Angela too, I imagine. They're the ones who burgled the house, looking for the money I already had. After getting the neighbors conveniently out of town for the night."

"Dad?" Dwight again, shocked and accusing. "You burgled a house? Angela?"

Angela only made a helpless gesture, but Henry leaped to the occasion. "I knew Franklin had that money hidden somewhere, and I'd eliminated every other place I could think of over the years. Now that he was dead, it belonged to me."

"And Barney Dorfmeier, don't forget," Jackie reminded him.

"Who the living hell is Barney Dorfmeier?" Dalton wanted to know.

"Was," said Jackie, shaking her head sadly. "An old friend of your father's—ninety-one years old, to be precise. Henry killed him this morning."

"Killed him?" Dalton's eyes opened wide.

"That's right."

Dalton regarded Henry with a bit more respect. "Who is he, and why is he saying my money belongs to him?" he asked Jackie.

"His name is Henry Hockersmith. He used to be a judge in this town, if you can believe that. He's also an old friend of your father's, or maybe 'friend' isn't exactly the best word for it. You might want to think of him as a former business partner." She watched Dalton's confusion deepening. "Winnie didn't happen to tell you where the money came from, did she?"

"No," said Dalton, thinking back. "She just said Jackie and Frances had the money—one hundred and fifty thousand dollars—and that it was safe."

"I wish it were safer," said Jackie with a sigh.

"So where did the money come from, exactly?" Dalton asked her.

"This is going to come as a bit of a shock, Dalton, so brace yourself. Your father robbed a bank," Jackie informed him.

Dalton stared at her.

"Excuse me," Henry put in, releasing one hand and signaling for attention. "He didn't exactly pull it off single-handedly."

"Correction," Jackie amended. "Your father robbed a bank with Henry Hockersmith and Barney Dorfmeier. Put your hand back, Henry."

"You're trying to tell me that three doddering old men pulled a bank heist?" Dalton asked. "You've got to be joking."

"What's that, brother?" Claire asked, sensing that the conversation had taken another important turn without her.

"Never mind, Claire," said Dalton impatiently.

"Doddering!?" Henry sputtered. Jackie waved him off with her free hand.

"They weren't always old men," she told Dalton. "Before you were born they were young and strong and full of harebrained ideas, like how to rob the First Central Bank of Palmer. Of course that was way back in June, nineteen twenty-seven."

Dalton paused, doing the math. "Seventy years ago," he breathed.

"And the really amazing thing is that they got away with it, too. The only problem was that the currency changed soon after that, and they were stuck with a fortune in worthless money. It was years before it was even worth selling as a collector's item. That's how your father helped support himself and Winnie since his retirement, and helped support Judge Hockersmith and Barney Dorfmeier, too."

"Oh, my God," said Dalton, his face beginning to go

gray. "I had no idea about any of this. I didn't think my father had any assets besides that house. He never told me."

"You may not have been high up on a list of people he'd trust with that kind of information," Jackie suggested.

Dalton swallowed, and seemed to be thinking about getting sick. "I made some bad investments, you see—got some people angry at me." He stopped, looked at Jackie as if begging her to understand something important. "I needed money so badly. If I'd only known about this, I wouldn't have had to . . ." His voice trailed off.

Suddenly, Jackie felt like she did understand, and she didn't want to. "You wouldn't have had to what, Dalton?"

He looked at her, mouth working, but the words wouldn't come out.

"You wouldn't have had to kill your father," she said, very quietly.

CHAPTER 28

Henry gasped. "*You're* the one who killed him? I thought it was just a stupid accident!"

Dalton shook his head. "I'd been calling Dad and begging him to sell the house and give me the money so I could cover some of my debts. He refused, of course. Winnie was going to get better and come home from Forest View, he said, and he told me they'd live out their days in that house. He told me I'd have to find another way to come up with the money I needed."

And he certainly had done that all right, Jackie thought.

"I flew into town a few weeks ago when it was getting windy, and the weather report predicted heavy rains. I climbed up on the roof while Dad was out visiting Winnie in the evening and ripped loose a few shingles—dropped them off the roof where he'd be likely to see them, on the side next to the empty house next door. I tore a pretty good-sized hole in the tarpaper, and pried one of the roof boards loose." He flexed his free hand as though he was remembering the unaccustomed hard work.

"That night I slept in my car, parked in front of the empty house. It rained, like the weather report had said it probably would, but towards morning it stopped. When I woke up, Dad was dragging a ladder around to the side of the house to fix the roof. The sun wasn't even up yet, and he was already going up there to take care of it.'' A note of admiration crept into his voice.

"You knew he'd try to fix it himself, of course," said Jackie. "He always fixed everything himself, didn't he?"

"Even when we were just little kids," said Dalton. "Dad was always good around the house. Mother never faulted him for that." He paused, looking almost sentimental.

"What's that, brother?" Claire asked. "What about Daddy?"

"Why don't you speak up a bit so Claire can follow along?" Jackie asked. "Or does she already know?"

Dalton swallowed. "She doesn't know," he said.

"What?" said Claire.

"Shut up, for God's sake!"

"So did you follow him up on the roof and throw him off?" Jackie asked.

"No," said Dalton. "If I'd had to face him I'd never have gone through with it. I hid back behind a hedge where he couldn't see me, and waited for him to start to come down. When he climbed onto the top of the ladder, I jumped out and pulled the bottom of the ladder out from under him. Then I ran for my car and drove back to the airport."

"You never looked back," said Jackie—a statement rather than a question.

"I was terrified!" Dalton declared. "What if he wasn't dead? What would I do then? But he was. Ed Woodrow, his next-door neighbor, called and told me. The phone was ringing when I walked in from the airport. Then I told my creditors their payment was guaranteed if they'd just be patient with me a little longer. I waited nearly a month before I came back to Palmer to sell the house."

"Afraid you'd seem too eager?" Jackie inquired.

Dalton nodded. "Only now I can't sell the house until I sink thousands of dollars I don't have into fixing it again."

"And you still need the money to repay your creditors."

"That's right. So hand it over now, and I won't hurt you."

"Oh, where have I heard that before?" Jackie lamented. "I don't believe you, Dalton. Henry, do you believe him?"

Henry snorted. "Not on your life. He'll kill us all."

"Yeah, well you ought to know as well as anyone," said Jackie. "But right now he's the one threatening me with a gun." She reached down carefully and felt for the handle of the suitcase near her feet. She lowered her voice to a whisper. "At least he's not getting the other thing I found in the house, huh, Henry?"

Dalton snapped to attention. "Okay, I heard that. I know you found something else in the house. I want it. Now."

Jackie turned to Henry and fixed him with a meaningful look. "He wants it, Henry. I think you'd better give it to him."

"I suppose I don't have any choice," said Henry. He reached into his coat pocket, removed something small and dark, and threw it hard at Dalton. Dalton ducked away from the object, scrambled to catch it with his free hand, nearly dropped it, recovered it, and brought it up to his face.

"Awk!" he yelped, and threw both hands into the air. The gun and Henry's thumb went flying in opposite directions.

Everyone followed the flight of Dalton's gun through the air like a slow-motion movie, gasping in unison as it arced down and fell toward Claire's head where she stood with her back to the excitement again, examining the bottom of a delicate antique porcelain fruit dish. At the last possible fraction of a second, Claire stepped aside and set down the dish. The gun landed on top of it, shattering it into a thousand pieces. Henry howled in dismay.

Claire reached down and picked up the gun. "Brother, isn't this yours?" she asked. She looked at Dalton, whose hands were still in the air, and whose face was frozen in a mask of horror, staring at Henry Hockersmith's mummified thumb, which had fallen to the floor a short distance away. She looked at Jackie and Angela, who were pointing guns at Dalton.

Claire aimed the gun at Jackie, then at Angela. "Don't you hurt my brother," she growled.

"We wouldn't dream of it," Jackie assured her. "Put the gun down, Claire."

"Don't shoot me!" Angela begged her.

"Give it to me, Claire," said Dalton faintly.

Claire couldn't hear any of them, but she seemed to know there was a threat here somewhere, and she was determined to stand up to it. She waved the gun back and forth between Angela and Jackie, pausing now and again to point it at Dwight and Henry. She didn't seem to notice the kids, or perhaps she didn't think they were much of a threat, trussed up the way they were, so she didn't point the gun at them. Everyone else got their turn at being in Claire's sights.

For the first time since this whole thing started, Jackie was pretty sure she was going to be shot. "Oh!" exclaimed Angela as the gun barrel swept by her. "Oh, dear God!" moaned Dwight. "My Bavarian china!" sobbed Henry.

"*Claire*!" Dalton screamed at the top of his voice. "*Give me the gun*!" He held out his hand. Claire got the general idea. She took two steps toward him and handed over the gun. Dalton pushed her aside and pointed it at Jackie.

There was a brown-and-black flash on the other side of the window behind Dalton, then the windowpane exploded inward, showering him and his sister with shards of glass, and Jake's jaws were around Dalton's gun arm, biting down hard. "Aaghh!" he screamed, and the gun fell from his useless hand and skittered away from him on the wooden floor.

Claire took one look at Jake with his teeth sunk into her

brother's arm, and began to screech so loudly and shrilly that Jackie began to worry about Henry's crystal liquor decanters.

Tom Cusack walked in the open door. "Good boy, Jake. I'll take him now." He gave Jackie a wink, and smiled at Grania. "It's okay, sweetheart. No one's going to be hurt now."

Jake let go of Dalton and turned to Angela, growling low in his throat.

"Call the dog off, or I'll shoot both of you," said Angela, her voice shaking with fear. She stepped out in front of the two teenagers. A moment later she was flying toward Jackie, propelled by the stiff kicks they'd delivered to her backside as soon as she got within reach of their feet. Jake intercepted her trajectory with a leap, and snatched her right arm. She screamed as they hit the floor, and the gun dropped with a loud clatter.

"Don't even think about it," Jackie warned Henry and Dwight, turning Henry's gun in their direction.

Tom picked up both guns and tucked them into his belt before untying Peter and Grania, who rushed into their respective parents' arms. Henry and Dwight sat on the floor with their hands under them and their backs to the wall, and looked dejected. Dalton sobbed and held his arm. Claire continued to scream.

Angela sat up and sniffled, looking down at the burns the polished wood floor had made on her arms after shredding two long holes in her spotless cream silk blouse. "Hurts, doesn't it?" said Jackie, not entirely without sympathy.

Tom stood in the middle of all of them, taking it all in. He started to laugh as he looked at Jackie, shaking his head. "So what exactly did you have in mind for a *second* date?" he asked.

CHAPTER 29

"I can't believe you let all the exciting stuff happen without me," Frances said, shaking her head at her daughter.

"I was a little preoccupied with events," Jackie reminded her. She was finishing up final preparations for the big spaghetti feed she'd planned for days. Tom and Grania were there, deep in conversation with Frances about genealogy. Peter listened from the kitchen where he was watching the pot of boiling pasta, and tried to look interested, but succeeded mainly in looking at Grania.

"Let me point out to you, Mother," Jackie reminded her in a no-arguments tone of voice, "that none of this so-called exciting stuff would have happened if you hadn't had to go around sticking your nose into other people's business and then dragging me along for the ride."

"Well, I hope you're properly grateful," said Frances. "Think what a dull week it would have been otherwise."

"I'm grateful to both of you," said Winnie Swann, looking up from the jigsaw puzzle that was spread out in front of her on the dining room table. Frances had managed to get Winnie released for the afternoon so that she could join them for dinner. "I've got my money, and I'm going to get my house back. I am, aren't I?" she asked Frances.

"You are," said Frances, "for sure. So stop complaining

about every little thing, Jacqueline. Everything turned out well in the end.''

''Thanks to Tom and Jake,'' said Jackie gratefully.

Jake heard his name and looked up to see what he could expect. A ball of orange fur curled up between his front paws uncurled itself into a fat ginger kitten, which began to give Jake's nearest leg a thorough tongue bath. Jake withstood this with as much dignity as he could muster.

Jackie looked at the two of them and smiled. ''I think Charlie's going to be a good influence on Jake,'' she said. ''At least he'll stay clean, now.''

Jake whined and cocked his huge head at the kitten, who stood up between his paws and began to lick his face. Finally he seemed to give up his protest at this parental treatment by something so small, and settled his head back down to the floor.

''I had a feeling Jake might enjoy another animal in the house,'' said Tom. ''People aren't the only ones who get lonely.'' He looked up at Jackie as he said this, his eyes full of feeling, and smiled.

Jackie felt her heart give a little flip. She smiled back.

Frances unfolded a map of Ireland, and laid it down on the coffee table in front of Tom and Grania. ''Now if your people came from Meath, then Cusack is probably from *de Cussac*, a Norman family who changed their name to *Ciomhsóg* when they adopted Irish ways back in the late twelfth century and settled in that part of the country. On the other hand, if they're from Clare then you're probably descended from the *Mac Iosóg* family who were. . . .''

''Spaghetti's done!'' Peter called from the stove. He'd thrown a piece of pasta against the wall, and it had stuck tight, his favorite method for testing the relative doneness of spaghetti, despite Jackie's frequent pleas that he try biting through a strand, or simply setting a timer.

''Everyone grab a plate and some silverware,'' said Jackie, taking the pot off the stove, draining the pasta into a colander and adding a drizzle of olive oil before bringing it to the table in a wide, steaming bowl and depositing it next to the platter of hot garlic bread.

"There's milk in the refrigerator, and I've got a nice bottle of Merlot breathing on the countertop for the grown-ups, if they want any."

"Count me in for that," said Frances, getting up and grabbing a wine glass out of the rack under the cupboard. "So that snake Dalton actually killed his father to get a lousy few thousand dollars out of that old house," she said, getting back to the subject she was really interested in. "And Old Judge Hockersmith killed his college roommate over some other money that he couldn't even spend."

"Well, to be fair to Henry, though I don't see why I should," said Jackie, "his motive was more to protect his son's political career than it was to have the money. If Marcella, or anyone else for that matter, had managed to discover the secret of his brush with crime seventy years ago, Dwight could have kissed Jane Bellamy's leather executive swivel chair goodbye before he ever sat down in it."

"Well, he won't be sitting in it now," said her mother. "And Palmer will have another four years of Mayor Bellamy." She shrugged. "Maybe in four years, I'll run for the job myself."

"You've got my vote, Mrs. Costello," said Tom.

"Mrs. Costello was my mother-in-law," said Frances. "A Hegarty, from Derry. If you want me to answer, you'd better start calling me Frances. Or Mom," she added with a sly little smile.

"Mother!"

"Oh, calm down, Jacqueline—I'm only joking." She gave Tom a wink Jackie wasn't intended to see, but she did. She also saw him wink back. Peter and Grania exchanged a look. Jackie sighed. This was beginning to look like another losing battle. *Oh, hell*, she thought to herself, *if I'm just going to lose anyhow, why bother fighting?*

"Well, at least the police don't want the money, and Winnie'll be taken care of," Frances went on. "That's all I really wanted in the first place. I had no idea everything would get so complicated."

"When you're involved, Mother," Jackie said, "things can hardly stay simple."

"So have you had enough of playing detective now, Grandma?" Peter asked Frances.

"I wasn't playing, young man," she replied. "And next time I plan to be there for the wrap-up."

"Next time?" Jackie froze with a forkful of spaghetti halfway to her mouth. "Mother, there isn't going to be a next time. From now on the Palmer Police Department can handle any crimes that pop up around here."

Frances winked at Tom again. "She's said that before," she told him. "But I know my daughter. There's always going to be a next time."